PUFFIN BOOKS

Truth, Lies & Homework

Josephine Feeney was born and brought up in Leicester. She was one of eight children born to Irish parents who had migrated to England during the Second World War. She worked for six years as an English teacher in comprehensive schools in Hull and Rotherham, and specialized further to teach children with special needs in Mansfield and Basildon schools, before leaving teaching in 1991 to pursue her writing full time. Her play Dear Tractor has been broadcast on Radio Four. She is married with two children.

Another book by Josephine Feeney

MY FAMILY AND OTHER NATURAL DISASTERS

Truth, Lies & Homework

Josephine Feeney

PUFFIN BOOKS

PUFFIN BOOKS

Published by the Penguin Group
Penguin Books Ltd, 27 Wrights Lane, London W8 5TZ, England
Penguin Books USA Inc., 375 Hudson Street, New York, New York 10014, USA
Penguin Books Australia Ltd, Ringwood, Victoria, Australia
Penguin Books Canada Ltd, 10 Alcorn Avenue, Toronto, Ontario, Canada M4V 3B2
Penguin Books (NZ) Ltd, 182–190 Wairau Road, Auckland 10, New Zealand

Penguin Books Ltd, Registered Offices: Harmondsworth, Middlesex, England

First published by Viking 1996
Published in Puffin Books 1997
7

Copyright © Josephine Feeney, 1996
All rights reserved

The moral right of the author has been asserted

Filmset in Garamond

Made and printed in England by Clays Ltd, St Ives plc

For my husband,
Ian McKay

INTRODUCTION

'Find out as much as you can about your grand-parents,' the teacher said. 'Ask lots and lots of questions. Then go to the library and see how their stories fit in with the stories in the history books.'

I can so clearly remember leaning back in my chair, stretching my legs out and thinking, 'Easy!' My gran-dad had already told me all about when he was little, how he used to help out with the work on his mum and dad's farm in Ireland, how he used to play all sorts of tricks on his family and the neighbours.

But that was before I started prying. After that it wasn't easy any more. It all became complicated and confused. Grandad, my family and school – nothing was the same. And the trouble it caused!

Why did I think it would be easy? Well, grandads are all pretty similar and there's only so much that you can write about them. We're a normal, ordinary family. Or I thought we were. We're not any more.

It's hard to believe that it was just a few short weeks ago that we celebrated Grandad's birthday – he was seventy-two. Mum cooked a special meal for him.

Afterwards, Grandad stretched and then stroked his newly swollen stomach. 'Honest to God, Linda, that was absolutely delicious. Sure God knows, you're a mighty cook.'

'Thanks,' Mum said, smoothing the lace tablecloth under her plate. My dad asked if Grandad wanted an ashtray.

'Well, what finer way to finish such a grand meal than with a Woodbine,' Grandad said, addressing the whole table.

Mum's face creased up in a distasteful look. She thought that Grandad set us a bad example. 'Do you have to, Grandad?' she asked.

Grandad finished his stout and placed the empty glass on the table with some ceremony. 'Arrah, Linda, a Woodbine doesn't do any harm at all. Sure these kids are educated. They'd never smoke, would ye?'

My brothers, Chris and Dominic, and I shook our heads and Chris said that it was a mug's game.

But when we were all stretched out relaxing in the lounge, Chris asked if he could have a sip of Grandad's stout, 'Just to see what it tastes like.'

'Why not? It's the finest nectar you could drink.' Grandad offered the glass to Chris, smiling.

Mum dropped the Sunday paper she had been reading. She was annoyed. 'Don't be getting them into bad habits, Grandad.'

Grandad smiled mischievously, ignoring Mum, as Chris tasted the stout. Then Chris offered the glass to me. I screwed my face up in disgust. I could never understand why Grandad liked the taste of stout – it was disgusting. Chris passed the glass to Dominic.

'No thanks, Chris. I'm more a lager man, myself,' Dominic said, smiling.

'What, Dominic?' Mum snapped.

'Only joking, only joking!' Dominic said, holding both hands up as if surrendering. Chris, Grandad and I laughed at Dominic's teasing and even Mum couldn't help smiling.

It was warm and cosy in the lounge and the autumn gloom outside seemed to make us even more snug. As the afternoon wore on, Grandad dozed, his loud snores gently rattling the glasses on the Welsh dresser.

Looking back now, it's hard to believe how calm and peaceful things were then. Sometimes my mind wanders back to that Sunday and I remember how I felt about Grandad before I discovered the truth.

1

The truth about Grandad. Well, not all of it, just a part, a very small part, but I never would have known if something hadn't happened at school. None of us would have known.

Esme De Silva, my best friend, was waiting for me as usual at the school gates on Monday morning. We walked down the drive together, comparing notes about the weekend's activities and the homework we should have done. I've known Esme since nursery school and although we've fallen out hundreds of times over silly things, we've always stayed the best of friends.

Esme's dad came to live in England with his family about thirty years ago. They used to live in Kenya but they're originally from Goa in southern India.

'Good weekend?' Esme asked.

'Not bad. It was Grandad's birthday yesterday so –'

'You had a party?' Esme interrupted. Nearly all of Esme's cousins live near her and they always have brilliant birthday parties.

'Not really. He just came round for his dinner.'

'I love parties,' Esme sighed.

'What have we got first?' I asked.

'History!' Esme said with a flourish. 'Don't you remember? Sanders is giving us a surprise. I wonder what it is.'

'It won't be anything exciting,' I assured her. 'It never is. Teachers only say things like that to get you interested.'

'You never know,' Esme said hopefully. 'Sanders is a bit different to most teachers.'

Miss Sanders was always in a rush. This morning she dashed into the room with her arms full of books and sheets of paper. She placed them carefully on her desk on top of a small mountain of other books and papers. She had to balance the new pile carefully so that they didn't slip off the mountain.

'Morning,' she said brightly. 'Now then,' she continued, searching for a folder on her desk, 'I think, yes, 7N, isn't it? Yes . . . we're starting an exciting new topic this morning, aren't we?' Miss Sanders was beginning to panic. Her glasses steamed up and she began to pull at her long, curly hair with one hand. 'Where is that wretched file?' she said, half to herself. Miss Sanders is about the most disorganized teacher I've ever known.

'Is it the blue one at the bottom of that pile?' Esme suggested helpfully. We always sit close to the front of the room so that Esme can read the board.

'Oh, Esme, you're a genius. Thanks,' Miss Sanders said, easing the relevant file from her desk and then clapping her hands loudly. 'Now then,' she said, 'what does history mean to you?'

The question was followed by a long silence and then a hand crept up at the front of the room.

'No, no, I don't really want an answer. I want you to think about it for a few minutes.'

The outstretched hand shrivelled down slowly, eventually resting uneasily on its desk.

'Does it mean wars and kings and queens?' Miss Sanders asked again, and a few heads nodded. 'Does it mean Romans and Tudors and Stuarts?' A few more heads nodded. 'I thought as much. Well, good news, girls and boys! History is *much* more interesting than that. Now, what I want you to do is settle in your seats and I'll tell you all about it.' People began to shuffle, stretch out their legs and move their backs down the chairs.

'That's right,' she said, 'make yourselves comfortable. This is a story.' She walked to the board and wrote in really big letters, HISTORY. 'You see, if we break that word down, it becomes HIS STORY. And it's not just his story, it's also her story!' Then she wrote the word HERSTORY proudly on the board.

'Boys and girls, what I want you to know,' she was talking as if it was really important to her, 'is that history and herstory is not just the story of wars and battles and kings and queens. It's also the story of ordinary people – people like you and me!' She stopped and the class was completely silent.

For a few minutes Miss Sanders stared at her writing on the board. Then she started talking again. 'For instance, have you ever thought of what your parents and grandparents did when they were young? Have a look at this leaflet.'

She rushed round the room placing three or four on each group of desks.

WORLD WAR TWO
THE PEOPLE'S HISTORY

Almost everyone in Europe was affected in some way by the Second World War. Those who remember the years 1939 to 1945 have their own story to tell, and some of these stories have filled the pages of great history books. Other stories have yet to be told. This is where you can help.

• Do you know what happened to members of your family in the Second World War?
• Was your grandfather or great-grandfather a soldier or a sailor or perhaps an airman?
• What about your grandmother? How did she help the war effort? In the munitions factory, the Land Army or the Women's Army Corps?

FIND OUT!
We want to hear about the lives of **ORDINARY PEOPLE** during the war through the words of their grandchildren.

Be part of the **PEOPLE'S HISTORY**.
Talk to your teacher for further details.

MIDLANDS WAR MEMORIAL
MUSEUM

'Now then, 7N,' Miss Sanders said, flourishing the leaflet. 'Wouldn't it be great if we were able to collect together the stories of your grandparents and great-grandparents?' There was a general murmur of approval and nodding of heads from the whole class.

'So, this is what we'll do. This week I want you to make an effort to go to the library, either in school or in town, and find out what you can about the Second World War. Then start asking questions. Talk to your grandparents or great-grandparents. Ask them what they did. At next Monday's history lesson, we'll discuss what you've found out so far.'

'What happens then?' Esme asked, interrupting Miss Sanders's flow.

'Well, we'll gather all the stories together and send them to the Midlands War Memorial Museum where they will be collated into an exhibition and a book. Dead exciting, isn't it?' Miss Sanders searched our faces for evidence of interest and enthusiasm. She was greeted with more nodding and cries of 'Yes!'

'Right. Any questions?'

'I already know what my great-grandad did. He used to talk about it all the time,' Ruth Davies said smugly. That was typical. If Miss had asked us to write about a visit to the moon, Ruth would say that she'd been there before.

'Great, Ruth, so you have a head start on everyone else.' Miss Sanders spoke politely, although I'm sure Ruth annoyed her just the same as the rest of us.

'What if your grandparents are all . . .' Jamie

Stevens said, unable to finish his sentence. Poor old Jamie. His mum and dad are both about sixty – well, they're old, so he's never known his grandparents.

'Difficult one, Jamie. Can't you ask your mum and dad? What I mean is, talk to your parents, they'll probably know exactly what your grandparents were doing in the war. Any problems on that one, Jamie, just get back to me. We might be able to find you somebody to talk to.'

There was an excited buzz of conversation around the classroom as plans were made about when people would go to the library and when they'd see their grandparents to talk to them. 'When shall we go to the library?' Esme asked anxiously.

'I don't know.'

'Oh, I forgot. You go to your grandad's on Saturday morning, don't you?'

My parents took my brothers to play football on Saturdays so I went round to Grandad's.

'We could go on Saturday afternoon,' I said.

'Now then, everyone.' Miss Sanders clapped her hands loudly. 'If you look this way I want to show you something. Each one of you will be given a folder complete with notepaper, file paper and a pencil. In five weeks' time I want you to return these folders to me, filled with the People's History, the HIS STORY or HER STORY of your family during the war. Is that clear?'

With great ceremony, Miss Sanders placed a wallet folder on everyone's desk. 'No graffiti on these folders, please,' she warned.

13

That morning, thirty pupils walked out from Miss Sanders's room fired with enthusiasm and each armed with a folder full of paper, ready to interrogate elderly relatives.

I couldn't wait to see Grandad on Saturday.

2

'What did you do in the war, Grandad?' That was the very first thing I asked on Saturday morning.

'What? What are you on about at all?' Grandad was clearing the ashes from the fire in his back room. He shook the ash pan so loudly that it was difficult to make myself heard. I repeated the question. 'Well, which war are you on about now? The Korean war? The Vietnam war? The Biafran war? The Middle East war?'

'No, no, Grandad. You know, the Second World War.'

'Oh that,' he said, smiling. I showed him the leaflet Miss Sanders had given us. He read it quickly and then, silently, he handed it back. He turned back to his ash pan. 'What's it like now, Claire? What's the weather like?'

'It's raining, Grandad.'

'Is it wet rain, would you say?'

'What do you mean?' I said, smiling. Grandad had some of the funniest expressions.

'Wet rain. Will we get wet, do you think?'

'All rain wets you. Anyway, what about this thing, the People's History?'

15

'Yes, but some rain wets you an awful lot more than other rain. That's what I mean, Claire, when I say, "wet rain",' Grandad said, patiently.

'Are you going to help me, Grandad?' I asked, exasperated. 'I'm not asking for much and you'll know all the answers.'

'You see, if it was dry I was thinking we could go down to St Mary de Burrell Church. I had a great idea during the week. Let me see now . . .' Grandad walked out of the house and stood in the garden for a few minutes with his hands outstretched, looking carefully at the movement of the clouds. 'Looks to me like it's clearing up, Claire, so I thought we could go and do some brass rubbings. I popped in during the week to get one of those permits. They cost a few bob but it'll be worth it. What do you think?'

'Good idea, Grandad. What about this project for history, though? Will you help me?'

'C'mon, Claire. We'll talk about it down the town.'

'Will you help, Grandad?'

'I will. Now let's hurry and get started before the rain . . .'

'So what did you do in the war?' I asked cautiously.

'We'll do the brasses first and maybe then I'll tell you,' Grandad said, smiling.

The church was shut. 'Due to Vandalism', it said on the notice board. 'What'll we do now?' Grandad asked, without expecting an answer. He seemed so disappointed. 'They never said it'd be shut when I bought this blessed permit.'

'Why don't we have a look around the graveyard?' I suggested.

'Why don't we? Cheer ourselves up, hey, Claire!'

The gravestones were so old – some were from the fifteenth and sixteenth centuries. Some of them showed where children of four and five had been buried. It almost made me cry to think of them. 'Why do you think they died when they were so young, Grandad?' I asked.

'Oh, disease and poverty. The common cold used to kill people in those days. They didn't enjoy good health.'

'Imagine dying of a cold,' I said, absentmindedly.

'Listen here to me, Claire, why don't we make some rubbings of these gravestones?' Grandad suggested. 'Arrah, they're no different to brasses when all's said and done.'

'Do you think it's allowed?' I was a bit nervous about it at first. It didn't seem right.

Grandad looked around. 'There's no one here stopping us.'

He helped me to place the paper over the epitaph and then I got rubbing. The first one looked like this:

HERE LIES INTERRED

CATHERINE ROWAN AGED 14 MONTHS
WHO DIED MAY 16TH 1798

AND HER BROTHER

WILLIAM ROWAN AGED 4 YEARS
WHO DIED JANUARY 5TH 1799

I rubbed away with my new wax crayon, feeling really strange – almost as though it wasn't right to be doing this. Then after a while I stopped noticing that the paper was placed over a gravestone and I began to notice the intricate patterns the crayon was making at the edges of the rubbing.

Grandad sat on a bench close by and smoked a Woodbine. He never calls them cigarettes. Maybe he thinks they're less harmful if he doesn't call them cigarettes. As I rubbed away with the wax crayon I asked Grandad about when he was young, during the war. 'For history, remember?'

'History – bunkum!' Grandad announced, as though that was the end of the matter. Then he thought for a few moments, with his thumb resting just below his mouth.

'What about during the war, Grandad?' I asked. The question was met with a stony silence. Grandad looked all around the graveyard. 'Well?' I asked again.

'Another time, Claire.'

'We've only got a few weeks, Grandad – that's for doing all the research and writing it up in neat.' Once again, Grandad remained silent. Then, after a few minutes, he leaned forward on the bench and said, 'Did you ever hear of that song, Claire, "McAlpine's Fusiliers"?'

'No, Grandad,' I said, without turning from the gravestone. I felt a bit annoyed with him, as he seemed to be avoiding the subject again.

'Listen to this:

18

'"Twas in the year of '39,
the sky was full of lead,
when Hitler was bound for Poland,
and Paddy for Holyhead.
Come all you worker laddies
and you long-distance men,
don't ever work for McAlpine
or for Wimpey or John Laing.

'I was one of them you know,' Grandad said, pointing his Woodbine at me.

'What do you mean, Grandad? One of what?' I asked.

'I was one of McAlpine's fusiliers. Do you know, Claire, that song was written about the likes of me – "Down the glen came McAlpine's men with their shovels slung behind them."' Grandad was singing in a loud voice now.

'I don't understand, Grandad. What's so special about that song?' I said, interrupting his singing. I felt a bit embarrassed – it didn't feel right to be singing in a graveyard.

'Well, we came over to England in 1939, over from the west of Ireland ... there were no jobs there, you know, so we had to come over.'

'Were you in the army then, Grandad?'

'Not at all! Sure, McAlpine's fusiliers were the men who fought the tar and the brick!'

'What?' I was getting more and more confused.

'Well, McAlpine was a man who owned a building company and when young Irish men came over to this

19

country desperate for work, he took them on – constructing roads and all sorts of buildings. So you see, I was like a fusilier – which is a member of a regiment – McAlpine's regiment.'

'Is that what you did during the war then, Grandad? Worked for this McAlpine bloke?'

'For a while, oh indeed – like almost every other Paddy who stepped off the boat in Holyhead.'

'And then what did you do?'

I was just finishing my fourth gravestone rubbing, as I spoke, neatening the edges – I felt quite proud of my work of art. Suddenly, Grandad said quietly and firmly, 'Take the paper off there, Claire. There's somebody coming.'

At the far end of the graveyard, close to the vicarage, was a man in a long black cloak. Lifting the black material from around his feet, he set off towards us at a considerable pace. 'What the hell –' he shouted. Then he slipped on some wet leaves. When he got back up and started running again, I noticed a great streak of mud all down his long, black cassock.

'Come on, Claire,' Grandad said urgently. 'Leave your crayons. I'll buy you some more.' Grandad took my hand as we ran towards the City Gardens. I couldn't understand why Grandad was so frightened of the vicar.

'Come back this minute!' the man in black shouted. 'Come back you . . . vandals!' I felt so guilty as we ran from the graveyard. Still holding my hand, Grandad crouched behind a shrub in the City Gardens.

'Why did we have to run from there, Grandad? We'd got permission.'

'For the brasses.' Grandad was wheezing slightly as he spoke. By the time we reached a bench in the City Gardens he was really struggling with his breathing. 'What I mean ...' he said in between deep breaths, 'I thought it wouldn't be any harm ... Ah, sure – it's only the Church of England!'

'You shouldn't say that, Grandad.'

'What?' Grandad looked at me, amazed.

'You should have respect for all churches. Perhaps we should go and explain to that vicar.'

'We will not! Sure they're not proper priests either, and I don't care what fancy thoughts your mother has put into your head but that is only the Church of England!' Grandad said forcefully.

'Yes, but you should still have respect, Grandad, if you don't mind me saying,' I added quickly, realizing that I needed Grandad's full cooperation for the history project.

Grandad sighed and changed the subject. 'What do you want to do this afternoon?'

'I said I'd meet up with Esme. We need to go to the reference library to find out about the war.'

'Fine,' Grandad said. 'Fine. There's a good race on the telly so we might pop to the bookies' on the way home.'

'And then will you tell me what you did during the war?'

'I might,' Grandad said, as if he was miles away. 'I might.'

3

'Will you two girls please be quiet!' the librarian shouted at us. 'Why do you have to make so much noise looking for books?'

Esme had pulled out two books on the Second World War and the whole of the one shelf had collapsed. We tried to put them back quietly but another shelf had collapsed.

'It isn't really us,' Esme said apologetically. 'It's these shelves, they –'

'Oh, so we've got noisy shelves, have we? Maybe it's because they can't read the notice on that wall that says "SILENCE"!' She was so sarcastic. 'And another thing. Are the shelves eating as well?'

Esme and I started to laugh, then I realized she was referring to the soft-centred fruit sweet rolling around my mouth.

'Oh, I see what you mean,' Esme whispered. 'It's because she's diabetic,' she lied. I couldn't believe it. The librarian didn't believe her either – I could tell by the suspicious way that she looked at me – but she wasn't really equipped to test.

'What did you say that for, Esme?' I asked when the librarian had returned, scowling, to the main desk.

'She might have asked to see my card.'

'Don't be daft, Claire. Diabetics don't carry cards, just sweets or biscuits.'

'You shouldn't have said it, Esme.'

'Well, you shouldn't be eating in the library! I was only sticking up for you but I won't do it in future.'

'Ssh!' It was the librarian again.

'Let's look through some books, Claire. Help me carry these to the table, otherwise we'll get thrown out.'

There seemed to be stacks and stacks of books about the Second World War. Esme was all for carrying every single one over to the table and going through each one. 'That's enough now,' I said after we'd carried four armfuls.

'All right. Where shall we start?' Esme asked, looking at the enormous pile.

'Start by shutting up, sitting down and reading!' It was an old man sitting at the end of our table. He was making notes from a massive volume. He looked quite annoyed.

I picked books up from the pile and flicked through them but I couldn't concentrate. They were all so detailed and complicated. 'Shall we look for it in the encyclopaedia?' Esme suggested. 'It'll be easier to make notes from that.'

'I hate working from the encyclopaedia, Esme,' I hissed. 'All those long words . . .'

'I know, but we've got to start somewhere.' Esme tried to pacify me.

'Shut up!' the old man shouted, looking towards us

23

angrily. The walls seemed to ring with his shout. I felt as though I wanted to crawl under the chair. The librarian walked over swiftly.

'What's wrong now?'

'It's these two. Can't you throw them out? They're causing that much noise and all I wanted was a little peace and quiet to ... ' The old man pointed his pen at us as if it was a gun.

'Please calm down and stop shouting,' the librarian said, sternly, 'or you'll be the one who has to leave.'

'What? That's marvellous,' the old man said sarcastically. 'You youngsters make me sick – you've got everything but manners.'

'What are you looking for, girls?' the librarian asked in the same stern tone.

Esme gawped at the librarian. I pulled out the leaflet from the Midlands War Memorial Museum. She glanced at it and then handed it back.

'So what exactly do you want to know?' the librarian asked again. She was getting even more impatient.

'About ordinary people ... during the war. What they did.' Esme spoke slowly, as if she was giving directions to a foreigner.

'Right!' The librarian leaned across the table and selected a book from the enormous pile we had carried over. 'This is a good one, *Life in Wartime Britain*. Now sit down and read through it quietly.'

'It's so long, though,' Esme complained.

'See what I mean? See what I mean?' the old man fumed. 'No manners!'

'Look at this chapter – this will tell you what

happened to all the men.' The librarian thumbed through the book. 'And later on there's another chapter about the women.' With that she placed the book firmly on the table between me and Esme and then walked hurriedly back to the main desk.

I started to read the chapter she had shown us. 'What's conscription?' I asked Esme. She shrugged her shoulders.

'If we had conscription today we wouldn't have half the hooligans or vandals . . .' the old man muttered.

'Well – what is it?' Esme asked.

The old man's tone was becoming calmer. 'It's where all the men had to sign up for the army, air force or navy. Now then – get your heads down and get some proper studying done.'

'Thank you,' I said, quietly. I looked down at the book and read: 'Every able-bodied male between the ages of eighteen and forty-one had to register for conscription. This process began with the youngest . . .' Strange. When I had asked Grandad that morning if he'd been in the army he had said, 'Not at all!' It said here that all men had to join. I wondered what Grandad had meant.

On the way out of the library, Esme smiled at the librarian, trying to leave a good impression. 'There's a leaflet here for you girls,' the librarian said. 'Pass it on to your parents – it's been developed by the City Health Team.'

On the way out of the library we looked at the leaflet. It said, 'Coping with Diabetes'. Esme laughed.

For some reason, I just couldn't see the funny side of it.

On Monday morning the class was buzzing with excitement when Miss Sanders asked if we'd done any research yet.

'Yes, Miss. In fact,' Ruth Davies said, holding a whole file of printed notes, 'my dad allowed me to photocopy lots of pages from our set of encyclopaedias.'

'Good, Ruth. Have you read it through? What did you find out from your research?'

'Well . . . I haven't actually . . .'

'Ruth, the most important thing about using reference books is that you learn from them. That goes for all of you. Don't just copy things out from books, read and discover.'

'I have read it through, Miss,' Ruth interrupted. 'I just haven't made any notes from it yet.'

'Right. Anyone else?' Miss Sanders asked. No one seemed willing to volunteer. Miss Sanders carried on, regardless. 'From your reading you will be able to compare the history books with the stories that your grandparents and great-grandparents provide. I want there to be a backcloth to their stories. Do you understand what I mean?'

We all nodded, apart from Ruth, who said, 'Yes,' in a lingering way as if to sound more intelligent than the rest of us.

'So, for this coming week I want you to spend some time researching with books and some time questioning your grandparents and great-grandparents. Any problems with that?'

No. No, when Miss Sanders spoke like that it sounded exciting, interesting and very straightforward. I couldn't wait to begin.

By the following Saturday I was wishing that I'd never started.

4

When I went round to Grandad's on Saturday we set off straight away for town. We were going to a dancing display.

It was amazing to watch my grandad dancing. Set dancing – whirling around the floor with seven other people in a set. Every now and again, when he was in a big spin, he'd let out a big 'whoop' just like we did on an exciting ride at Alton Towers.

After a few minutes I noticed that Grandad wasn't the most gentle dancer. Some of the women winced as he waltzed them round, his shoes missing the floor and landing on their feet instead.

'We're doing the Kerry set this morning,' Grandad shouted out at me and his friend, Roddy. Then he apologized for breaking yet another set of toes as he stepped out of place.

'Isn't he a great man?' Roddy announced. He wasn't really talking to me – he was sort of talking to himself and shouting above the music.

The music and the heavy dancing rocked the floor so much that I almost felt as though I was standing on a ship. There was a final great 'whoop' before the dancers and the musicians stopped as one. Each group of dancers sort of fell towards one another, laughing and patting one another on the back.

'Jeez, you were absolutely brilliant!' Roddy said to Grandad as he walked towards our table. He was. I couldn't stop smiling at him.

'D'you fancy a pint, Roddy? They're opening up the bar any minute,' Grandad asked when he'd got his breath back.

'Indeed I do!' Roddy said. 'It's awful thirsty work, watching.'

'What about yourself, Claire? Would you like a lemonade and a bag of crisps?'

The musicians started up again as soon as the bar was opened. They sat in one corner and played slow, lingering airs that seemed to calm the dancers. 'Do you see this man?' Grandad asked between huge gulps of the cool, black stout. 'This man saved my life many years ago, Claire.'

'How do you mean, Grandad?'

'Do you know, Roddy, Claire is writing my life story. It'll be put on display in a museum too, you know. Isn't that right, Claire?'

'Well, sort of.'

'What are you writing about your grandad then?' Roddy asked.

'I'm writing his story – history, do you see?'

'Well, indeed I do! And what a story. Your grandad's family were great neighbours of ours, Claire, and didn't we leave Kiltimagh, County Mayo, together, on the same train? And haven't we always been pals, even more so since the day we set foot in this country – McAlpine's fusiliers?' Roddy said.

'You know, Claire, when we came over in 1939, the war was about to start. We had no idea. We worked all over the place – buildings, roads, whatever, wherever. Then the call-up came.'

'What do you mean, Grandad?'

'Well, they needed men to fight and every man between certain ages was to go to war. So we had to present ourselves for the army or the navy –'

'Or the air force.' Roddy finished the sentence for my grandad. 'But your man here had other ideas,' Roddy continued. He was smiling so broadly.

'Arrah, the war was nothing to do with me anyway,' Grandad seemed to be reminding Roddy.

'But you went about it the wrong way altogether,' Roddy protested. They seemed to be going over an old argument. I couldn't understand what they were talking about.

''Tis easy for you to say that now,' Grandad said, pointing his half-full glass of stout at Roddy.

'Grandad, I don't know what you're on about,' I said quietly. 'I'm completely lost. What happened when you went to join the army?'

'He didn't. That was the problem,' Roddy said. He looked quite solemn.

'What do you mean?'

Grandad leaned towards Roddy as he spoke. 'Whatever happened about the call-up, I ended up in prison,' Grandad said, half-smiling.

'What?' I couldn't believe my ears. I thought he was joking at first.

'It's true, Claire. Your grandad was in prison,' Roddy announced.

'What do you mean, in prison? Do you mean like a criminal is sent to prison? Like a thief or ... a murderer?'

Grandad leaned back. He had such a serious, thoughtful look on his face. 'Yes. Like a common criminal.' For a few moments Grandad and Roddy sort of stared into their drinks. Then they both looked around the room, and began to tap their feet to the musicians' rhythm. Before long they began talking about something else.

At that moment I felt so confused. This was terrible. There were so many questions running around my brain. I couldn't think clearly, I felt sick. Grandad was sent to prison. To prison? My grandad?

The floor seemed to be floating and the music was really, really annoying me. I just wanted to stand on my stool and shout out, 'SHUT UP!' in a booming voice. If everything was quiet I'd be able to sort this out.

Roddy and Grandad were miles away, years away. Even when Roddy went to the bar for more drinks and Grandad asked me if I was all right I felt as though he was on another planet.

It's so hard to describe how I felt at that moment. I suppose this is the best way: if you've written a really long story on sheets and sheets of paper, then before you've had time to put numbers on each sheet, somebody comes along and throws all the paper up in the air. When the sheets fall to the floor, you haven't a clue in which order they should be. That's how I felt –

31

and the music, talk and dancing were driving me up the wall.

I was so confused. Part of me was dying to know the rest of Grandad's story. Why was he in prison? How did he escape from prison? The other part of me wanted to run away and forget all about it. I know I shouldn't say this but I think I felt ashamed of him. Ashamed of my own grandad. My grandad, *my* grandad had been in prison, in gaol, in the nick.

It was at that moment that I wished I hadn't asked any questions.

5

'Give us a hug, Claire. I've missed you today, standing at the edge of that cold football field,' Mum said as soon as I arrived home. 'What've you been up to?'

'Nothing much,' I said. I felt like crying, I was so weighed down with Grandad's revelations.

'Phew! You stink of smoke, love,' Mum said holding me away from her. 'Where've you been?'

'The Cornmarket Centre. Grandad's been in a dancing display. Me and Roddy were watching. What's for tea, Mum?' I wanted to change the subject. I didn't want this thundering in my head, these questions.

'Grandad and Roddy! I suppose the stout was flowing freely and the air was filled with Woodbine smoke. That's no environment for you, Claire,' Mum said gently. 'Honestly, sometimes I wonder if your grandad has any sense at all, taking a child into that sort of atmosphere. You should have a word with your dad,' Mum called out to my dad, who was in the other room. 'Couldn't you meet up with Esme on Saturday, Claire?'

'It wasn't that bad, Mum.'

Mum wandered over to the cooker, freeing me to take off my coat. Even I could smell the Cornmarket

Centre bar on my clothes, reminding me of Grandad and Roddy's unnerving reminiscences.

Mum moved about the kitchen quickly, wiping down surfaces and sorting out saucepans. I watched her neat form as she moved about so efficiently and I so wanted to tell her what Grandad had told me, but the quicker she moved, the more I realized how shocked and appalled she would be.

'Mum . . .' I began.

'Yes, love.' She didn't look round.

'What did your dad do in the war?'

Mum stopped suddenly. 'Why?' she asked, almost in a whisper. Mum doesn't talk much about her dad. He died when she was about eighteen.

'For Miss Sanders's history project. I was just wondering . . .'

'Well . . . he was only eleven when war broke out in 1939 so he was still at school, and when the war finished in 1945 he was just sixteen. He'd started work in an engineering factory, making parts for the war effort, when he was fourteen.'

'So he didn't fight?'

'No,' Mum said gently as she sat beside me. 'He used to say that it was one of the greatest regrets of his life – not being able to fight because he was too young. Did his National Service in 1948, though.'

'What's National Service?' I asked.

'During the war, all men between certain ages and some women had to enlist, in the armed forces, to help fight the enemy. After the war, the government

34

decided to carry on for a few years, just to be on the safe side. It was called National Service.'

'How's the tea going, Linda?' Dad asked as he walked briskly into the kitchen.

'Fine. Me and Claire are just having a chat –'

'Come on, let's get it going,' Dad interrupted, chivvying Mum. 'We're all starving after standing outside for almost the whole day.'

'Claire's doing a history project and she was asking what my dad did in the war. What did your father do?' Mum asked Dad. I froze and yet I could feel my face on fire.

'Couldn't tell you,' Dad answered nonchalantly. 'I've never asked him. What's that noise upstairs?'

'I'll go and check,' I said quickly, wanting to be out of the kitchen. Dad didn't know about Grandad. I stood for ages in the hall trying to work out exactly what I should do. What would Mum think if she knew? What about Dad?

I decided that the best thing to do was to leave it for a few days, say nothing. Talk to Esme, see what she said. Yet I so wanted to tell Mum and Dad, just to tell someone.

'What is the noise, Claire?' Dad shouted from the kitchen as I sat on the bottom stair. I hadn't investigated. For the last few minutes I hadn't even heard it.

'I think it's Chris and Dominic arguing over the computer.'

'Honestly! Dominic is nearly sixteen – you'd think he'd know better – and Chris acts more like a four-year-old than someone of fourteen. Chris! Dominic!

Keep that noise down!' Dad shouted. They ignored him. I could hear their arguing.

'You said I could take over when I came out of the bath!'

'No, I didn't. Anyway, you've only been in the bath five minutes.'

'I don't care, it's my turn.'

'Grow up, you two!' Dad shouted again. 'Why don't you learn to compromise? You're always fighting.'

Fighting. Fighting. The words spun around in my head. What would Chris and Dominic say if they knew about Grandad? After Dad returned to the kitchen I sat on the bottom stair, toying with the idea of ringing Esme.

I tried to imagine my brothers' reactions. 'Ooh, really?' Chris would say, liking nothing better than a good, cosy gossip. 'Tell me more!'

Dominic's another matter. He seems to have everything sorted out and certain things have a great importance in his life. Like football. He'd probably say, 'So what?' Then again, he's talked about joining the army when he leaves school so he might be disgusted. Yes, Dominic's always finding things disgusting.

'Dinner's ready, Claire,' Mum announced from the kitchen. 'Tell your brothers, will you?'

Tell my brothers? No, I couldn't. Dominic would be disgusted and Chris would probably tell everyone.

'Claire,' Mum nudged me again. 'Be a love, tell Chris and Dominic that dinner's ready. Bit of peace all round.'

36

'Yes,' I muttered before climbing the stairs in a trance. Peace? If only I could tell somebody.

6

'My great-grandfather was a war hero,' Ruth Davies declared, reading from her immaculately typed project. 'During the Second World War he served with the Royal Engineers and in 1944 he landed with his regiment to liberate Italy from the Fascists. They landed at a little seaside place called Anzio which is a few miles from Rome.' Ruth smiled and looked all around at her entranced audience.

I hated Ruth Davies. She was the smarmiest, creepiest creature in the whole world. Why was it that her great-grandfather had to be a war hero? Why couldn't he just have been an ordinary soldier or sailor? She'd always been like this. More frills on her party dresses, more fondant fancies in her birthday tea, more Barbie doll outfits than anyone else. Esme looked at me and raised her eyes to the ceiling. She shared my thoughts on Ruth 'whatever-you've-got-mine's-bigger' Davies.

'That was a marvellous introduction, Ruth,' Miss Sanders said, clapping her hands together as if in applause. 'Tell me, what's that brown thing on your desk?' Esme and I sniggered.

'This, Miss Sanders,' Ruth said dramatically, 'is a detonator from a mine which my great-grandad actually defused. It takes pride of place in our home, as we never forget his heroic exploits on our behalf.'

I could just picture the scene in Ruth's house: 'Anyone seen the detonator lately?'

'Is it safe?' Jamie asked, looking nervously towards the brown thing.

'Jamie,' Ruth said condescendingly. 'It's a German detonator – it's been made safe and it would need some explosives to detonate and seeing as we haven't got any – '

'You never know these days,' Jamie interrupted. 'What with all the terrorists . . .'

'Now we're getting a bit off the subject here,' Miss Sanders said quickly. 'Has anyone else started their his or her stories?' The room fell silent. 'Esme? Claire?' Miss Sanders looked straight at us.

'No!' I snapped. There was no way that I would stand up here and read out Grandad's story. No way would I tell Ruth Davies and Co. that not only was my grandad not a hero, no, worse than that, he was in prison during the war. As soon as Miss Sanders asked me I had made up my mind. I wasn't telling anyone, ever.

By break-time I couldn't stand it any longer. I felt that I desperately wanted to tell someone, just so they could say, 'Oh, how awful for you!' So I talked to Esme.

I didn't tell her straight out. It's not that I don't trust Esme. I just wanted to know what she'd think.

'Esme, how would you feel if one of your family was sent to prison?' I asked.

39

'What?' she asked, surprised by my question. I repeated it. This time she looked more thoughtful. Then, she began digging. She always does this. 'Why, Claire? Has someone in your family been caught doing something?' Then she giggled. It wasn't funny but I had to be careful not to give too much away. So I pretended that it amused me, too.

'No, no. It's just that I was watching something on telly and I started wondering what I would think if, say, my dad was sent to prison.' I don't think I was very convincing. I asked her again. 'Go on, tell me. How would you feel?'

'At first I'd feel dreadful – you know, ashamed. I wouldn't want anyone to find out,' she said thoughtfully. 'But then it depends . . .'

'What do you mean, "it depends"?' I asked.

'Well, it depends what they've done. If they'd done something dreadful, like murder, I wouldn't want to know them any more.' Esme thought for a while and then she continued. 'But if it was for something they believed in, like protecting a swan's nest from road builders or something . . .' Her voice trailed off.

'Would you tell anyone?' I asked.

'I suppose that depends too, doesn't it?'

'Not here it doesn't. People make fun of you for the least little thing,' I said.

'Yeah, you're right. I probably wouldn't tell anyone. You'd get called awful names like "gaolbird". People are horrible sometimes, Claire.'

'I'd hate anyone to know,' I said quietly.

'Know what?' Esme asked.

'Oh, nothing. I was just thinking about that programme.'

Esme looked at me closely. Then she pushed me in a playful sort of way. 'Go on, tell us,' she said. It was hard to resist Esme when she was so persuasive. Her voice dripped with secrecy and intrigue. 'You know I'll never tell anyone, I'm brilliant at keeping secrets.'

So I told her. Well, there wasn't much to tell, just what I'd heard from Grandad and Roddy after the set dancing. I spoke slowly and I looked at my hands. There wasn't much to say but it made me feel less confused as I spoke each word out loud: 'My grandad was sent to prison during the Second World War.'

'God, Claire!' Esme said in a low voice.

'You won't tell anyone, will you, Esme?'

'No, I said I wouldn't. You can trust me.'

'It's just that, well . . . I'd hate anyone here to find out. Promise you won't say anything, Esme?'

'Promise,' Esme said. She put her hand over mine as if to reassure me. 'That's what best friends are for, Claire.'

7

'I can't do it, Grandad. I can't do this project!' I said loudly the following Saturday.

'Why not?'

'Because – well, look at this leaflet, it says: "Was your grandfather or great-grandfather a soldier or a sailor or perhaps an airman?" You weren't any of these, Grandad, and I can't very well write down that you went to prison, can I?'

'And further down here, my girl, it says: "We want to hear about the lives of ordinary people during the war through the words of their grandchildren," so – '

'But you're not ordinary, Grandad. How many ordinary people go to prison?' I said, despairing. 'And we've only got two weeks left. Ruth Davies has already nearly written a book.'

'Suit yourself,' Grandad said, as if he couldn't care less.

'Don't be like that, Grandad. Help me! What am I going to do?' I said, pleadingly.

'Do you want to help me to transplant some early winter cabbages?' Grandad asked, smiling. Sometimes it infuriated me when Grandad was like this.

'Grandad, please!'

'Have you talked to your mum and dad about this?' Grandad asked.

'They're too busy. Mum told me a little about her dad but he was only very young during the war. Dad's really busy with the union at the moment.'

'And your brothers?'

'They're no help – they're just obsessed with football.'

'And the bold Esme?' Grandad said, smiling.

'Esme? Well, she's a lot of help. Do you know, Grandad, I told her last Monday about you and Roddy. I made her promise not to tell anyone about it and what do you think was the first thing she did when we saw Miss Sanders?'

'She told her?'

'No! She made me tell her! I was so furious. Then Miss Sanders got all excited and asked if you were a conscientious objector.'

'So what did you say?'

'I said that I didn't know. Then she was saying, "This is fascinating, this is fascinating." I could have choked Esme.' Even as I told Grandad I still felt angry towards Esme. After seeing Miss Sanders I really shouted at her that she wasn't to be trusted. I even walked away from her. I didn't think it was worth being her friend any more.

'I never told her – you did!' Esme had shouted after me.

'You made me, Esme!' I shouted back.

'I don't make you do anything. You could have told Miss Sanders that you didn't want to talk about it.'

43

'Oh, yes, I'm sure I could, Esme,' I had said sarcastically. On and on it went, until Esme eventually agreed that she had broken her promise.

'Sorry,' she had snapped in a voice laden with defeat. Things were a bit cool between me and Esme for a few days after that.

'Are you still friends though?' Grandad asked quietly, breaking into my thoughts.

'Sort of. What am I going to do, Grandad?'

'About Esme?' he asked mischievously.

'No! About this rotten project? Why couldn't you have been ordinary and just joined the navy or the air force? Not everybody got killed, you know. I've been reading about it, Grandad.'

Grandad moved from his armchair and into the kitchen, where he clattered around putting the kettle on and then searching for cups and spoons. 'Do you want tea or hot chocolate, Claire?'

'Hot chocolate. Were you a conscientious objector, Grandad?'

There was a long silence. I moved over to the stool close to the kitchen door. Grandad's eyes scanned the shelves backwards and forwards as if he was searching for an answer.

'Do you know what conscientious objectors are?' he asked solemnly.

'Sort of,' I lied.

'They're people who think very carefully about whether it's right or wrong to fight in a war or to help the war effort. They decide it is wrong and so they face the consequences. Very few of them went

44

to prison in the last war, you know, Claire. Most of them took jobs that were left vacant.'

'And is that what you did, Grandad?'

'It was not. I was eighteen when I came over in 1939 and I was that carefree, sure I hadn't a notion about anything apart from where I'd get the next meal, Woodbine and glass of stout. I hadn't a clue about the war.'

'So why did you end up in prison?'

'Would you like a nice bit of flapjack with your hot chocolate, Claire? I made a pile of it yesterday. It's a wonder there's any left at all – '

'Grandad,' I said urgently. 'Why did you end up in prison? Please tell me.'

Grandad moved about steadily, making the drinks and prising the sticky flapjack from the tin. 'I'll tell you the story when I'm sitting comfortably with my tea, flapjack and Woodbine. So you get your paper and pen ready and stop rushing me, girl.'

This whole project was making me bad-tempered. Even the syrupy flapjack didn't improve my mood, as Grandad seemed to take an age over positioning the ashtray, Woodbines, matches, flapjack and tea. He was like somebody preparing for an important task. By the time he was ready to tell me I was ready to scream. Why couldn't he be ordinary like everyone else's grandad? Why did he have to be different?

'Do you see your Dominic?' Grandad began. 'How old is he?'

'Sixteen,' I said quietly, trying to conceal the angry impatience.

'And what's he like?'

'Why? What's this got to do with Dominic, Grandad?'

'Well, I'll tell you what it has to do with Dominic. I was just a year or two older than Dominic when I came to this country. Dominic's football-mad, isn't he? He still argues with Chris like a child and he still likes your mum to make his sandwiches. All those years ago I was just the same.'

'But that isn't why – '

'The letter came one morning and I read it along with the rest of the lads, all Irish, in a boarding-house in Nottingham. We had a good laugh at it and then I tucked it behind the clock on the mantelpiece. Sure I can still see that old clock now.'

'What did the letter say?'

'I can't remember the exact words. Well, honest to God, it was first thing in the morning and I'd had a skinful of stout the night before. I think it said that I had to report to some army base or other. Well, says I, I have better things to do.'

'And then what happened?'

'Then, a couple of weeks later, another letter came. Same sort of thing, only this time it said that if I didn't report to such and such a place I would be arrested.' Grandad took a deep swig of his tea and lit a second Woodbine.

'So what did you do, Grandad?'

'I ran away!' He spoke with a mischievous smile as if he'd done something really amusing.

'You ran away?' I asked, finding it hard to believe

what Grandad had said. 'Why?' For ages Grandad stared at the smoke he'd just exhaled. 'Why, Grandad?' I asked again, as if to remind him. 'Why did you run away?'

'Like I said, I was only eighteen – sure I hadn't a serious notion in my head. "What'll I do?" I asked one of the other lads sitting there at the table. "If you're not here, they won't know where to find you," he said. So, I says, "Well I might as well take off then." A few of the lads sitting around the table said, "Good on yer!" and that was it. I packed my small bag and took off.'

'Where did you go, Grandad?'

'Not far.'

'Where?'

'Arrah, Claire, I can't remember to tell you the truth,' Grandad said, lifting himself slowly out of his armchair. 'It wasn't far enough, anyway. What about a bit of flapjack?'

'What do you mean, "It wasn't far enough"?'

'Do you know something, Claire, you're wearing me down with all these blessed questions!' Grandad walked over to the window and looked out towards the winter cabbages. 'I was caught and dragged back to face the court. *That's* what I mean, Claire, when I say that it wasn't far enough.' Grandad didn't look at me as he spoke. He stared out at the neatly arranged garden for a few minutes before finally stubbing out the Woodbine and walking quickly back into the kitchen.

No matter how hard I tried I couldn't imagine

Grandad tucking the second letter behind the clock in that Nottingham boarding-house and then running away. I just couldn't picture him running anywhere with his small bag of belongings.

Grandad on the run and then sent to prison. What a story! What would Ruth Davies say when she heard this? What would my parents say?

Butterflies seemed to flutter about my stomach. I felt so excited at the thought of Grandad's story and very curious to know what had happened next. And yet . . . I felt strangely worried. What would everyone say when they heard about Grandad running away, getting caught and being sent to prison? What would they say?

8

'Get much of your project done?' I asked Esme, first thing Monday morning.

'Yeah, loads. What about you?'

'Not much. Grandad told me a bit, but he's so slow and I still didn't find out much about it. If only we had more time.'

'Listen,' Esme said after a long pause, 'I've got an idea. Why don't we skip Art this afternoon?'

'What?' I asked, horrified. 'I'm not truanting.'

'It's not really truanting. The teacher never notices whether we're there or not so she won't notice that we're missing.' Esme was so persuasive.

'I don't know, Esme,' I said, still cautious.

'Go on, Claire. This project is much more important than Art. Go on – no one will miss us.'

'I'm not sure.'

'Go on,' Esme whispered, just after the teacher clapped her hands for silence. There was no time to answer.

My stomach was churning over and over all morning. At dinner time I told Esme, 'I don't know if I'll be able to go, Esme. I think I've got the runs.'

'Don't be daft, Claire,' Esme said dismissively.

49

'You'll be all right. There's loads of toilets in town.'

'But what are we actually going to do? Go to the library?' I hissed, like a reluctant spy.

'You'll see,' Esme said, full of intrigue and mystery. I decided then that I would go with her. After all, nobody would miss us. The teacher never even noticed when we were there.

Escaping from school was easy. We walked out of one of the back doors and through the park at the side of the school. No one noticed us. We got off the bus near the court and crossed over by the big council offices. There weren't many people in town, mainly office workers with neatly folded umbrellas rushing for an early bus home.

'What if I see my mum?' I said, thinking aloud.

'You won't – she'll still be at work,' Esme reassured me.

'But what if she decides to nip into the fish market?'

'She won't,' Esme said with some finality. 'It's closed on Mondays.'

We walked along past all the bus shelters at the top of Welford Road. We were walking out of the town centre.

'Where are we going?' I asked Esme urgently. 'Tell me!'

'You'll see in about two minutes,' Esme said. I hated this – she was acting like a know-it-all teacher or parent.

Most of the buildings on Welford Road were boarded up and empty. There were posters over the boards advertising pop groups I'd never head of and a meeting to discuss getting the government out. I wanted to be back in the safety of the big town shops, with piped music and bored assistants. Where was Esme taking me?

'Here we are!' she announced. Her arms reached out to the grey stone front towers of the prison. I couldn't take it all in. I kept staring at the enormous grey towers and the red brick walls reaching up to the sky. They started from the pavement, just as if they were bricks belonging to an ordinary house or shop.

'What are we doing here, Esme?'

She looked at me as if I had asked a really stupid question. 'It's the first part of our investigation.'

'Good,' I said quickly. 'Now that we've done that, let's go back to town.'

'What?' Esme said. She was looking at me in a really strange way. 'We haven't done anything yet, Claire.'

'What are we going to do then?' This was getting a bit silly.

'I thought we could ring the bell and ask if we could speak to the governor – he's the person in charge. Then we'll ask him if he's got any record of your grandad being here during the war. Then we could ask him why your grandad was in prison.' Esme pointed to a different finger as she spoke her list of things to do at the prison. It couldn't be this easy, could it?

'I'm not sure about this, Esme,' I said, looking up at the grey stone towers. 'Don't you have to write and ask for permission first?'

'No, I don't think so. Look, there's a bell next to that big notice. Why don't we ring it and see?'

'Esme, we shouldn't be doing this. They might tell our parents.'

'They won't. We're not doing anything criminal,' Esme said as she walked towards the doors.

'Don't, Esme,' I pleaded.

'Why not? Look, Claire. I'm only doing this to help you.'

'I know, Esme, and I do appreciate it, but it just doesn't feel right, you know, going behind Grandad's back –'

'We're doing it *for* your grandad.' Esme was pleading with me now. 'Come on, Claire, don't spoil things now that we're here.'

'I'm not spoiling things. It just doesn't seem right.'

Before I could protest any further, Esme rang the bell.

'Esme!' I shouted. 'I don't believe you've done that.' I started to back away. I wanted to run as fast as I could so we wouldn't be caught ringing the bell on this big front door of the prison. 'If we ran now,' I thought, 'they'd think it was just two kids messing about.' At the same time I was transfixed with curiosity, almost longing to know what would happen next.

Esme rang the bell a second time. 'They're obviously busy,' she said impatiently. Suddenly, the small door built into one of the enormous front gates opened with a slow, creaking sound.

'What's this? Avon calling?' It was a man dressed in uniform, probably a prison officer.

'No,' Esme said curtly.

'What then?' The man looked as if he'd just been awoken from an afternoon nap. 'Come to visit your dad?' he asked, spluttering into a nasty laugh.

'No!' I said angrily.

'We'd like to see the governor, please,' Esme said in such a snooty fashion.

'You what?'

'Your boss. The person in charge,' Esme said, looking beyond the man as if he was an insignificant butler at the door of a great mansion.

'My boss?' he asked. Then he started to laugh again. 'What for?' he said between guffaws.

'We'd rather discuss the matter with him,' Esme said. 'It's confidential.'

I'm sure Esme didn't mean to sound rude but I could tell by the man's face that he no longer found the episode funny. 'For your information, ladies,' he began in a different tone. 'I am the boss of this part of the prison so if you've anything to ask me, get on with it. I do have a lot of other responsibilities to attend to.'

His sternness silenced us and it seemed as though we had both forgotten why we were there.

'You explain.' Esme nudged me back to reality.

'What?' I took a deep breath before I could continue. 'Me?' I asked Esme. 'But it was your idea.'

'Go on, explain, Claire,' Esme said between closed lips.

'Oh, don't mind me,' the man said. 'I can listen to you all day. Don't start fighting, though.'

'We wondered,' I began hesitantly, 'if we could have a look at your records, please.'

'What?' he bellowed. 'What for?'

'Well, we know someone who was in prison during the war and we wanted to find out what they were in for. If you don't mind. If it's not too much trouble.'

The man folded his arms above his rounded stomach, leaned back and looked at us for absolutely ages. Esme and I waited anxiously for his response.

'It's for a project,' Esme said quietly.

The man seemed to be searching for the right words. 'Never, ever in my twenty-two years of service at this prison have I ever known kids to have the audacity to even ring that bell. But not only do you ring the bell and ask to see my "superior", you also want to see the prison records. Well, all I can say is, I don't believe it.'

'It's true, honestly, we know this person very well –' I began.

'Not that!' he bellowed. 'Talk about stupid!'

Esme and I looked at one another as if to check that he was really talking to us. 'In my twenty-two years of service,' he said again, 'I have never, ever known two such cheeky young people – to come up to the main prison gates and ask to see our records as if it was a public library or something. I suppose next you'll be wanting to check the cells.'

'That's a good idea,' Esme said, completely oblivious to the man's rage.

'God, kids today. They've absolutely no respect!' With that the man retreated behind the door of the prison and before either Esme or I could say anything else he slammed it in our faces.

'What a horrible man!' Esme said, sticking her tongue out at the prison door, which was ringing with the sound of the slam. 'I'd hate to be a prisoner in there if he's in charge of the gate.'

'Oh, Esme, what are we going to do now?' I asked desperately. For once Esme was silent. She turned and started to walk back towards town as if she'd run out of ideas. I followed, quietly trying to work out how we'd explain our absence from school and just how I could finish this wretched project.

9

During the six weeks' holiday I sometimes get frustrated when my parents are so busy with their jobs that they don't have time to do things with us, apart from our two-week holiday in Wales. Now, it was different. I was really glad that Mum and Dad were fully occupied with their work. They didn't ask too many questions and they never really noticed that things weren't quite right.

'We're on opposite sides in a different situation at the moment, Claire,' Mum explained when I arrived home late on the Monday evening. 'So your dad and I would be very grateful if you'd keep any disruption to the normal routine to the absolute minimum.'

I wasn't quite sure what Mum was on about but I said, 'OK,' in all the right places. Mum is a personnel officer in a knitwear firm and at the moment she was sorting out redundancy packages for a third of the workers. On the other side of the fence was my dad, who's a trade union official, acting on behalf of some of the people losing their jobs.

'We're trying not to bring our work home,' Dad said as we sat around the table for tea. 'But it's difficult for both of us at the moment, so if we're late back or a bit short-tempered, try to understand.'

Chris and Dominic nodded wisely. They were so understanding that they waited until after tea to taunt me about being missed at fire practice and holding the school bus back for twenty minutes so I wouldn't miss it.

'Where were you?' Dominic hissed. 'You've had it tomorrow!'

Tomorrow. My stomach churned over all evening as I thought about facing the consequences of the prison visit.

'You'll never guess what,' Esme announced excitedly first thing Tuesday morning. It was as though yesterday hadn't happened. 'We missed all the fun yesterday. Did you know there was a bomb scare?'

'Fire drill,' I corrected Esme in a flat voice.

'No, no. It was a bomb scare. Jamie's mum rang up the fire brigade because she was so concerned about Ruth Davies's detonator. She told them it was an unexploded World War Two bomb and so the whole school was evacuated! What a laugh!'

'We were missed, Esme.' I couldn't see the funny side of yesterday's events. Esme wasn't listening.

'God, I bet Ruth Davies was well embarrassed. She had to assure the fire brigade that the detonator was really safe. Bet she isn't in school today,' Esme continued. 'This'll wipe the smug smile from her face!'

But for once I knew how Ruth Davies must have been feeling. It was an awful day.

'Me and Esme are in trouble,' I told Grandad that

evening. Mum and Dad were going to be late home from work again so I had asked if I could go to Grandad's to work on my project.

'Make sure your grandad brings you home – the streets aren't safe after dark now,' my mum cautioned, over the phone.

'What have you been up to?' Grandad asked while pouring himself a glass of stout. 'C'mon, tell your old grandad. I'm sure it's not half as bad as you're making out.'

'It is, Grandad.' So I told him all about me and Esme truanting from school so that we could go to the prison, and how Miss Sanders had been absolutely furious that two of her class had dared to truant, and how a letter would be sent home, and how Mum and Dad had asked us to be good, and . . . and . . .

Grandad listened attentively, although every now and again he coughed as though he was trying not to laugh. When I'd finished he wiped his eyes and said, 'Sure jeez, that Esme is some character when she talks you into doing that, isn't she?'

'Well, it's just that, if you don't mind me saying this, Grandad, you seem to be taking ages to tell me about why you were in prison and there's so much I don't understand. I'm getting a bit fed up with it so I thought I'd go along with Esme. I didn't agree with her at first but I couldn't think what else to do.'

Grandad sat looking at the backs of his hands and his disintegrating Woodbine for ages. The smile and the sparkle had gone from his face and he looked saddened at what I'd said.

58

'Even Jamie has found out some of his grandparent's story and they're not even alive.'

'Well, for a start, Claire, you would have had a hard job finding me in any prison records in Leicester as I was in Lincoln Gaol. Then, I suppose another thing – when I was eighteen I couldn't have cared less but now, now that I know so much more about what was going on . . .' Grandad's voice trailed away into silence again.

The doorbell rang loudly, shattering the peace of Grandad's back room. 'That'll be Roddy,' Grandad announced with relief. 'Let him in, will you, Claire.'

Roddy came to see Grandad most evenings. They would have a glass (or two) of stout together, watch a bit of the old telly and play the odd game of cards.

'Can you remember, Roddy, the exact reason why I was sent to prison? Claire wants to know a good bit more and sure my old memory is creaking under the weight of stuff.' Grandad and Roddy had switched the television on and turned down the sound, providing a flickering light in one corner of the room.

'Was it for non-payment of council tax?' Roddy asked mischievously.

'Get out of that, Roddy! Sure council tax only came in these last few years.'

'Maybe you didn't pay for your beer money – in that pub where you used to put everything on the slate!' Roddy and Grandad laughed uproariously at this answer.

'Sure Claire, we do have great crack here together in

the evenings,' Grandad said as if he'd forgotten my request.

'No, I'll tell you, Claire,' Roddy said, becoming suddenly serious. He did. At last I had something to work on. I knew exactly why Grandad was sent to prison. It wasn't anything dreadful or criminal, yet the way that people reacted, you'd have thought he'd killed Churchill himself.

10

Why? Why did I read it out? I should have had more sense. Why did I listen to Esme's nagging, cajoling voice. 'Go on, it's dead interesting. Miss Sanders might forgive us for the other day if you read it out.'

I listened carefully to the other stories. My stomach churned over and over as the details of men who had travelled to Africa or airfields in Lincolnshire to defend the country filtered into my mind. One minute I was thinking, 'Yes, I'll definitely read it,' and then when I heard about another hero who rescued hundreds of people I changed my mind.

Then Jamie stood up to read. He cleared his throat twice before he said, 'My grandfather's story is a bit different.'

'Fine, Jamie. We'd love to hear it, so, whenever you're ready . . .'

'My grandad walked from southern Italy to England in 1931. He was looking for a better future for his family – '

'Walked?' Ruth questioned, as if Jamie was making it up.

'Ruth! Manners, please. We don't interrupt one

another. These are very personal stories,' Miss Sanders said harshly.

'Yes, he walked. There was no money for bus or train fares. He came to Leicester and after working for a while in a factory he saved up enough money to open a little shop. When the war broke out they said that my grandad was an enemy so they closed down his shop and sent him away to a camp on the Isle of Man. Some of his friends from home weren't so lucky. They were put on a boat to go to Canada. The boat was torpedoed and it sank. They weren't the enemy. They had never done anything wrong.'

Jamie sat down. As he noticed Miss Sanders's questioning face he added, 'That's as far as I've got, Miss.'

'That's excellent, Jamie. Lots more to find out there. Very well done. We look forward to hearing more of that story,' Miss Sanders said, as she walked purposefully around the front of the classroom. She hadn't asked, as she normally does, if there were any questions. It was almost as though she was protecting Jamie from the condescending remarks of Ruth, among others.

'Anyone else want to read theirs?'

There was a long pause. Most people had read the first part of their story. Esme nudged me. 'Go on,' she whispered.

'No,' I said firmly.

Even so, I was thinking about how Jamie had confidently read out his grandad's story. He wasn't a hero, I thought. People said he was an enemy. That wasn't any worse than my grandad. 'OK, Miss, I'll read the first part of mine,' I volunteered, surprising even myself.

'Good, Claire. Which reminds me – I need to see yourself and Esme later, about the other day.'

'Shall I start?' I asked, trying to distract Miss Sanders's attention.

'Yes, go ahead.'

I stood up and cleared my throat several times. This was it. I tried to sound confident, as though there was nothing to apologize for. Jamie had managed and nobody had said anything. I looked around as if to check my audience. They all seemed to be ready to listen sympathetically. Apart from Ruth. She looked challengingly at me as if to say, 'Let's hear if your grandad was as much of a hero as mine.' I wanted to knock the back legs off her chair. Instead I read proudly and confidently:

'My grandad went to prison during the war. Before you start thinking he was a thief or a murderer, he wasn't. It was something completely different.

'In 1939, when he was eighteen, my grandad came to live in England. He didn't want to, he had to because he couldn't get a job in Ireland. Still, he looked on it as an adventure. He wanted to earn enough money so that he could buy a farm in Mayo, where he came from.

'Unfortunately, just before my grandad came to England war had broken out. One of the first jobs Grandad got was helping to build a new runway at an air force base. He was living in a boarding-house in Nottingham with some of his friends.

'Because of the war, all men were called upon to sign up for the army, navy or air force. After a while a letter came for my grandad asking him to report for a medical check-up. This was to see if he was fit enough to go and fight for his country. Grandad didn't think that England was his country so he ignored the letter. He didn't really know what the war was about.

'A few weeks later Grandad received another letter. It was a warning letter. He was told that if he didn't turn up for his medical he would be in trouble. Grandad was frightened so he ran away. Eventually he was caught and sent to prison – all because he didn't turn up for his medical check.'

I sat down quickly. 'Well done, Claire, a very good start,' Miss Sanders said, thoughtfully. 'It's wonderful to have such a range of stories – '

'I don't believe that,' Ruth remarked, interrupting Miss Sanders.

'Will you have manners, please!' Miss Sanders warned.

'You don't get sent to prison for not turning up at the doctor's!' Ruth sneered, all the time looking around for support. A few heads nodded.

'Ruth – I am getting a little tired of your impolite interruptions. Now will you please be quiet!'

The class was shaken by Miss Sanders's anger. There was lots of shuffling and nervous coughs.

'After all, these are the precious stories of your grandparents and great-grandparents. You shouldn't be questioning whether they're true or not. It has been great to hear Jamie's and Claire's contributions this morning – it gives us all a different perspective on the war, doesn't it?' A few heads nodded. 'So, let's listen with courtesy and respect – and no more impolite questioning. We can follow up these latest accounts next lesson.'

Not everybody waited for the next lesson for the follow-up. In the crowded dining-room I noticed Ruth sitting across the table from Dominic, smiling prettily and telling a 'You'll never guess what . . .' tale in the sweetest way. Dominic's face changed. I couldn't hear what she was telling him and the rest of the table but I could guess. He stood up quickly, packed his sandwiches away and stormed furiously out of the dining-room.

Why? Why had I read out Grandad's story? I had never realized that it would cause so much trouble.

11

I knocked loudly on Grandad's front door. He was taking ages to answer. 'Grandad! Grandad! Are you there?' I shouted. After a few more agonizing minutes the door was eventually opened. Grandad looked dreadful, like he'd just woken up. His face was all grey and badly creased with red sleep lines.

'Well, jeez, that must be some monster pursuing you when you're so desperate to come into your grandad's house.' Grandad was smiling but I had the feeling he was a bit annoyed about being disturbed.

'Grandad,' I said quickly, 'can I have my tea here? I've made a terrible mistake.'

'What in the world are you on about?' he said, closing the door behind me.

'Grandad, I read out your story,' I said while walking into the back room, 'and it seems to have all gone wrong.' As I spoke Grandad eased himself into his armchair and searched for a Woodbine and a match.

'How do you fancy a bit of sausage, bacon and egg, Claire? I don't know about you but I'm starving,' he said, exhaling the first mouthful of smoke. Then he coughed – a rasping, hacking cough that bent his back forward.

'That's bad for you, Grandad,' I said, momentarily forgetting my own troubles. Grandad just smiled, his knowing smile that seemed to say, 'How many times have I heard that before?'

While Grandad loaded the frying-pan with sausages and bacon, I sat on the stool at one end of his small kitchen and told him about the terrible day.

'I read the story, Grandad, and Miss Sanders thought it was great. Ruth Davies said I was a liar but she got told off for that. Then at afternoon registration she said, "You are a liar. I asked your brother and he said it was nonsense." Then she said, "And even if it is true, I think it's disgraceful." Esme swore at her. It was a terrible afternoon, Grandad. I'm so fed up.'

'Ah sure, take no notice of them. Wait'll you taste these delicious sausages. They're a new recipe.'

'Grandad – sausage and bacon can't make things better!' I said impatiently. I felt guilty immediately, as Grandad was only preparing the tea for me. 'Do you know what happened after school? Dominic, my own brother, threatened me. He said that he'd heard that I'd been telling stupid stories about you and if I didn't stop, he'd sort me out.'

'What did you say then, Claire?' Grandad asked, turning each sausage a little to one side.

'I told him it was the truth. That you and Roddy had told me, and then he kept saying, "I'm warning you, I'm warning you." Honest, Grandad, he was just like a thug.'

'What about Chris? Where was he when all this was happening?'

67

'Chris came along eventually and said, "What's up, what's up?" like he does in a real gossipy way, so Dominic told him. But you know Chris, Grandad, he was just going, "Tell me more, tell me more." There's nothing Chris likes more than a bit of scandal. I was so fed up with Dominic that I walked off. I didn't even catch the school bus. I hate Dominic's nagging.'

'Do you want to ring your parents, so?' Grandad asked, placing two plates carefully on the grill to warm.

'They're working late. They've said we've got to try to keep things running smoothly. Oh God, I'm so fed up. Why weren't you ordinary? Why did you have to be different? If only you hadn't ignored that letter.'

At that moment I couldn't even look at him. My kind grandad who was filling the kitchen with delicious smells and chopping mushrooms carefully to put alongside the sausage and bacon. I felt so, so angry at him for putting that letter behind the clock. Why did he have to do that?

'Now then, do you want this egg runny or hard?' Grandad asked, ignoring my pleas for his ordinariness.

'I'm not that hungry,' I said, even though I was famished. I wanted, in some way, to sort of punish him.

'Huh! My girl, you'd better be,' he said sternly. 'For I'm not eating ten sausages and eight rashers tonight!' Grandad never did things by half. I didn't have much choice.

A few minutes later, after a big gulp of tea and half-way through the sausage and bacon, Grandad laid his knife and fork carefully on the plate. 'You see, Claire, people often say things like that when they don't know the full story. Dominic hasn't a clue, really, what was going on then. When you finish writing it and your classmates know the full story, they'll think differently, I promise you that, Claire.'

'How did you feel, Grandad?'

'When?'

'When they said you had to go to prison.'

Grandad chopped his bacon carefully and opened the top of his egg as if allowing the yolk to escape. It was funny how he always seemed to concentrate on little, unimportant activities before he answered my questions.

'Well, how do you think?' he said as he carefully chewed the egg-soaked bacon. 'At first I was a bit proud, you know, convinced that I'd done the right thing, but then . . . I suppose more than anything else, I felt ashamed. I used to think, "What if my mother and father found out? What would they say?" They wouldn't have been proud. They didn't understand what was going on. You know, when I left Ireland, Claire, they said to me, "Be a good lad, above anything else." Ah sure, it's a long time ago now.' Grandad's shoulders fell forward as if he had a great sadness, like a heavy rucksack, to carry. I knew he didn't want to talk any more.

He pushed his chair back carefully and walked over to the sideboard. 'Which reminds me, Claire,' Grandad said quietly. 'I've been meaning to show you this.' He placed a small, sepia photograph beside my plate.

'What's this?'

'That's myself and Roddy, standing outside the old house in Mayo the day before we left for England. I found it the other day – I thought you might like it. I'm telling you, that brings back some memories.'

'Can I stick it at the front of my project?' I asked, hopefully.

'Why not? They'll see who you're writing about then.'

'I haven't done much yet, Grandad.'

'Sure, Claire, your project will be as good as the next one's. Don't be worrying about it.'

'I'm not sure about that, Grandad. I've only got nine days left. Will you help me this Saturday? I've got to get it finished.'

'Why wouldn't I, Claire? Now – how do you fancy a nice cup of tea and a couple of fig rolls?'

I laughed at Grandad's solution to every big problem – bacon, sausage, egg, flapjack or fig rolls. 'What about Dominic? What am I going to say when I go home this evening?'

'Tell Dominic to take a running jump and stop being so flaming pompous,' Grandad said dismissively. 'Sure God knows what your mother gave him when he was a baby for him to turn out like this.'

12

Dominic's threatening looks darkened the whole house when I arrived home. 'Where've you been?' he asked like a crabby teacher.

'Grandad's.'

'For more stories?' Dominic said sarcastically. He was lying sprawled across the settee, watching an American agony aunt encourage people to pour out their hearts. Without taking his eyes away from the tear-stained television faces he said, 'You're in trouble when Dad finds out what you've been saying!'

'Dominic,' I said forcefully, sitting to one side of the television so he'd have to look at me, 'you don't know what you're talking about.'

'What do you mean?' he said, dismissively.

'If you knew the whole, true story you wouldn't be acting like this.' I sat, waiting for him to respond, but he kept his eyes fixed firmly on the television. 'I can't understand why you're so – '

'Tell me then!' he snapped.

'What?'

'Tell me all about Grandad's story.' The way he said it made me feel as though I could have slapped him. It was true what Grandad said, he was so pompous.

'You won't listen properly, Dominic. You think you know everything.'

'I'm listening, Claire. Go on, tell me.'

'Well,' I began. I told him as much as I knew and all the time I was talking I felt so uncomfortable. Dominic's face was crossed with the most disbelieving sneer. At times he nodded his head as if I was talking rubbish.

'You are so naïve, Claire,' Dominic said when I finished. 'You are the one who doesn't know anything. Do you know what this means? All this story – do you realize what it makes Grandad?'

'No.'

'It makes him a traitor, Claire!'

'Don't be so stupid, Dominic, and don't call me naïve!'

'You see? You know nothing,' he said, swinging his body round to sit straight on the settee, ignoring the American agony aunt who seemed to be demanding our attention. 'Do you know what went on in the Second World War? Hasn't Miss Sanders told you all about Hitler?'

'Yes, a bit,' I lied.

'And did she tell you what he did to the Jews and the gypsies and even some Catholics like us? Did she? Did she? You see, you're so naïve! Did she tell you how they were killed in concentration camps?'

'She told us a bit about it,' I lied again.

'And that's why we went to war – to stop all that. Thousands of brave people fought and died to stop Hitler and you think Grandad was a hero because he was too chicken to fight? You're pathetic, Claire – and you're even more pathetic telling everyone at school about it.'

'It wasn't like that, Dominic. Grandad wasn't too chicken! He didn't know what to do.'

'No, he didn't,' Dominic said, angrily. ''Cause he's Irish, isn't he?'

'That's got nothing to do with it, Dominic.'

'Oh God, Claire, you're so thick! I've had enough of this. I'd rather do my homework than listen to this rubbish.'

'But what do you mean about him being Irish? What do you mean?' I asked, desperately.

'You see? You don't know a thing and yet you spread stupid stories about our family around school, just so it looks good. I'll bet any money that Grandad didn't tell you that Ireland was on the same side as Hitler during the war. Did he tell you that, Claire? No, I thought he didn't – and that's probably why he went to prison – because he was a traitor!'

With a righteous smirk Dominic walked confidently out of the room. I settled back in the chair, thinking about what Dominic had said and half-watching the television. The glamorous American woman sat close to a member of the audience and held the microphone at a sympathetic distance.

'We were such a happy family once,' she sobbed into the microphone. 'Then it all went wrong.'

'Do you want to tell us about it?' the caring voice said, off camera.

'No!' I shouted at the television. 'I'm not telling

anybody!' The tear-stained face and sympathetic microphone ignored me so I switched them off and watched the dot disappear.

I wasn't naïve – I hated being called that – but I didn't know who was on whose side during the war. When Dominic talked about it like that it almost sounded like a silly playground argument. Taking sides.

Grandad had never said anything about whose side he was on. I'll ask him on Saturday, I thought. We'll be able to clear this up and I'll prove to Dominic ... Prove what? Prove that Grandad was telling the truth? Prove that Grandad wasn't a traitor?

At that moment I wasn't sure what I was supposed to be doing any more, what I was supposed to be looking for. Miss Sanders had asked us to find out the story – the his or her story – of what our grandparents had done during the war. I'd never realized that history – Grandad's story – was so complicated. Why couldn't it be straightforward like Ruth Davies's or Esme's?

13

Later that evening Mum and Dad returned in a celebratory mood. 'It looks as though we've almost settled things, Claire,' Mum said, wrapping herself around me in a big hug. I was glad they were back home. I'd felt so lonely all evening and I couldn't concentrate on my homework. 'We'll have to do something special this weekend. As a family! Celebrate a return to near normality.'

'I'll need to go to Grandad's on Saturday, Mum. Sort out this project.'

'Oh, Claire, surely that can wait. Wouldn't it be lovely just to be together as a family for the day?' Mum said, sipping the sparkling wine Dad had poured for her.

No, it wouldn't. 'And Grandad's not all that well.'

'He's fine,' Dad said, smiling.

'Just doesn't look after himself, Claire,' Mum added, stroking my frown. 'Don't you worry.'

'He's a creaking gate, be around for years yet.'

'He drinks too much, smokes too much and eats terrible fried food. Bad for the heart – but will he listen?' Mum said, dismissively.

'And Roddy's not a great influence on him,' Dad

75

said, as if Grandad was a fourteen-year-old involved with a gang of bikers.

'The project needs to be handed in soon and I've hardly started,' I said, trying to remind Mum and Dad about why I was really going to Grandad's.

'Mmm,' was all Mum said in reply. There was a long silence. I could tell they were both very tired.

'Have you finished the redundancies yet?' I asked.

'Almost,' my dad said, looking downhearted. 'We shouldn't really be celebrating, Linda.'

'No, you're right. It's not exactly a great occasion – but our work's very nearly done, Sean.'

'Yes.'

'And they've all got good packages,' she said, as if persuading Dad.

'No jobs, though,' he said with a deep sigh.

'Don't worry about your grandad, Claire,' Mum said brightly, changing the subject quickly before Dad became more morose. 'He'll be all right and you'll finish your project. You've always been a good worker.' The wine was going to Mum's face, reddening her cheeks and brightening her eyes.

If only it was that simple. If only they weren't going to be astonished and annoyed when they read Grandad's story.

'Don't worry, don't worry,' Mum said again, continuing to stroke the frown that seemed ingrained on my forehead. 'Now, let's see what Dominic and Chris are up to?'

The ice-cold lump grew in my stomach. Dominic, would he tell them? If they heard it from him first, they wouldn't get the right story. He didn't know the full story.

'Please don't say anything, Dominic,' I implored in my head. 'Please wait – at least until I've finished my project.'

14

'Lovely!' Miss Sanders clapped her hands together and smiled enthusiastically at the whole class as Esme sat down. 'I'm so thrilled at the way all of you are tackling this project. There have been so many brilliant stories and we haven't finished yet.'

Esme seemed to grow about five inches in her chair. She'd just read about how her grandad had helped to defend Kenya from a German invasion. Ruth, as usual, interrupted by saying, 'But Kenya's thousands of miles from Germany!'

Esme threw one of her famous withering looks and Miss Sanders merely had to say, 'Carry on, Esme. Take no notice of any interruptions.' Esme continued even more confidently, describing the war days in an African country.

'Which reminds me,' Miss Sanders said, changing to a sterner tone. 'I have heard, on the grapevine, that some of you are taunting others about these stories. Is that true?' After a short pause she continued, 'It would be most unfortunate if this project was ruined by prejudice and bigotry. So, no more unkind comments and Ruth, please, although you've got a very inquiring mind, please, no more interruptions. OK?' Ruth nodded reluctantly, and chewed her lip.

'She sounds like a fine teacher, Claire,' Grandad said when I told him about the lesson.

The day was closing in quickly over Grandad's back garden. It was so peaceful, all we could hear was the constant hum of the distant motorway and Grandad's muttering as he battled with the whitefly. 'Sure it's no weather for Brussels sprouts – they've been eaten alive by the rotten whitefly.'

'Whose side were you on, Grandad?' I asked as he angrily uprooted a whole stalk of the sprouts.

'When?' he said impatiently, putting the good sprouts in a bowl near our feet and casting the bad ones towards the compost heap.

'In the war. Dominic said that Ireland was on Hitler's side.' Then it all poured out – the things Dominic had told me about the concentration camps and how Grandad was a traitor because he was Irish. For ages Grandad worked at pulling out the sprout stalks as if he was furious. 'Grandad?' I prompted him gently, 'Were you on Hitler's side?'

'I was not!' he replied angrily. 'And neither was Ireland. Ireland was neutral!'

Grandad sounded so cross. But at least now I knew and I'd tell Dominic: Ireland was neutral; Grandad wasn't a traitor. If you don't take anyone's side in the first place, you don't betray anyone.

I followed Grandad back to the house and sat on the back doorstep as he changed out of his work boots.

79

'Do you want sausage and bacon, Claire?' Grandad asked.

'No thanks. Mum says I'm not to eat fries. They're bad for my heart.'

'Well honest to God. Since when did your heart digest bacon, sausage and egg, hey? They might be bad for your stomach but – '

'After your stomach,' I tried to explain.

'Ah sure, Claire, you'd eat nothing if you listened to the so-called experts!' Grandad kicked his boots angrily into the shed. 'What about your dad? What has he to say about all this?'

'What do you mean, Grandad?'

'Have you told them anything about me being in prison during the war? Or Dominic. Has he said anything?'

'I haven't said anything. I'm not sure about Dominic.'

Grandad became calm again and lit a Woodbine. He blew the smoke out in one unit until it landed halfway up the garden. I watched it so closely that I almost forgot what we were talking about.

'Come on, Claire, let's go for a walk,' Grandad announced. Then he quickly and forcefully stubbed the Woodbine into the ground. 'I read about passive smoking this week, Claire. It's an awful thing. Maybe I should give up the old Woodbines.'

'Dad doesn't know, does he?' I asked carefully.

'About passive smoking? Arrah, I'm sure he does – isn't it in every paper at the moment?' Grandad was smiling.

'No, no. About the prison. He doesn't know. Mum asked him the other day what you did in the war and . . . why doesn't he know, Grandad?'

'Get your coat, Claire. We'll go for a walk – I'll tell you while we kick the leaves around Owlton Park.'

The leaves had drifted into the corners of the park. There were a few lining the footpath as we walked slowly along towards the swings and the climbing frame.

'When your father was a young man, Claire, a few years older than yourself . . .' Grandad spoke without looking at me, '. . . my brother died. I hadn't seen him in years. We got word that he was going to be buried up in Bradford. Your dad came with me to the funeral and afterwards there was a reception in a pub near the church. The church was packed – I'd never seen anything like it. Anyways, afterwards the priest came up to myself and your father to sympathize. "I'm sorry for your trouble," he said. "Despite his problems and his lifestyle, he was a great man." "Problems?" says I. "Well, with him being a man of the road and all that," the priest says.'

'What, a lorry driver?' I interrupted.

'Not at all! He was what you used to call a tramp. He had only enough money in his Post Office savings book to pay for a funeral and to buy his mates a few drinks afterwards. He had a great wake.'

'A tramp?' This was hard to believe. My dad's uncle, my great-uncle, was a tramp. If he had lived in Leicester he would have probably sat in the pedestrian

81

subway near the museum asking for loose change. What a dreadful thing.

'Well, they wouldn't call him a tramp nowadays. He'd be called a vagrant or a homeless person or –'

'Was he homeless?' I asked.

'He was.'

'Why? He could have come to live with you.'

'Ah, like so many, it was the drink. He had everything, but he was always sad about having to leave home, so he took to the drink. I suppose it gave him some comfort. Anyways, the thing is this – on the way home your father says to me, "I have never felt so ashamed in my life. Today I discovered that my uncle was a tramp. I'm so ashamed."'

I wasn't sure what to say, so I just looked beyond the trees and the swings to the traffic racing along the darkening ring road. Grandad went quiet – he wasn't even kicking up leaves any more.

'Anyways, I says to your father, "There but for the grace of God go I."'

'What does that mean, Grandad?'

'It means, Claire, it could easily have happened to me. Sure, becoming homeless can happen to anyone. Well, that day I said to myself, "If this is his attitude, I'd better not tell him anything about my sojourn in prison."'

'So you didn't tell my dad?'

'I didn't.'

'So Mum and Dad don't know?'

'They don't,' Grandad said finally.

15

There was something that was still puzzling me. Even though Dominic was pompous and annoying he'd made me think. If Grandad had known about the Jews and the gypsies, why didn't he fight to stop Hitler? Why did he decide that it wasn't any of his business? Why did he go to prison where he wouldn't be able to help anyone?

I had wanted to ask Grandad the day before but he was just so cross when I told him about Dominic. He was furious that Dominic had said he was a traitor. I didn't want to upset him even more.

'What do you think, Esme?' I asked as we sat on the low wall at the side of the playground eating our packed lunch.

'Maybe he didn't know,' Esme said brightly.

'But what about the papers? Grandad always reads the papers.'

'Maybe it wasn't in the papers,' Esme said in between mouthfuls of chocolate biscuit. 'I know how we could find out!' Esme said, as if she'd been miraculously struck with an idea.

'No, Esme. No more skiving from school.'

'No! I've got a brilliant idea. Why don't we look at

the local papers from 1939? They keep them, you know, in the library.'

'We haven't got time, Esme. The project has to be handed in a week today and I've got to find out the rest of Grandad's story tomorrow.'

'Let's ask Miss Sanders if we can go during a lesson. She'll understand.'

'What?' Miss Sanders asked disbelievingly.

'It's just that we're both a bit pushed for time – '

'Esme, we still haven't sorted out the last time you truanted and now you're asking me to give you permission to miss lessons.'

'Not exactly, Miss,' Esme said, diplomatically.

'What do you need to know that's so urgent? Can't it wait until tomorrow?'

'No,' I said flatly. Esme smiled at my honesty. 'You see, Miss, my grandad needs to tell me the rest of his story tomorrow so that I can hand it in next Friday so we haven't got time to go to the library then.'

'What exactly are you looking for?'

I explained. I told Miss all about Dominic – what he'd said about how Grandad was a traitor and how he hadn't helped those people who were killed by the Nazis. 'I want to prove to Dominic that Grandad wasn't a traitor,' I said firmly.

'But that's not school work, Claire.'

'It's all to do with the project, Miss,' Esme said, defensively.

'What exactly are you doing, Claire? Are you writing your grandad's story or – '

84

'Writing Grandad's story.'

'Fine – in that case, you find out what your grandad did, write it down and hand it in. It's as simple as that. You've done your background research – now get on with it!' Miss Sanders said firmly.

I was quite shocked at her sternness. 'But what about Dominic?'

'That is your problem. You and Esme are not having time off to solve your family problems. And we still need to sort out the truanting.' Miss gathered her papers and started to leave the room. Then suddenly, she turned. 'Apart from anything else, Claire, Dominic is talking nonsense. People did not find out about the concentration camps until the war was almost over. Those who enlisted and were conscripted did so because they didn't want their country to be invaded!'

'Are you sure, Miss?' Esme asked.

'Esme – you are really pushing your luck! I suggest that both of you get on with your project and have them ready to be handed in next Friday. I don't want to hear another word about libraries or extra research. For goodness' sake, you're doing a history project, not writing a historical novel!' With her spare hand Miss Sanders drew her hair back off her shoulders and walked angrily out of the room. On the way she brushed past Ruth.

'Trust you two to put her in a bad mood,' Ruth said snootily, as she sauntered towards her desk carrying a large cardboard box.

'Oh, why don't you go and invade Italy again,' Esme shouted screwing up her face.

'Typical!' Ruth said, even more snootily. 'You don't even know that my great-grandfather and men like him didn't "invade" anywhere. They liberated Italy. But then, I wouldn't expect you two to understand!'

'What's in that box?' I interrupted, trying to change the subject. Ruth had placed her large cardboard box on her desk. As she spoke to us she checked the contents as if examining a Christmas hamper.

'My project.'

'Already?' Esme questioned. 'But it's not due in for ages yet. What've you brought it in for?'

'Because I've finished writing it and I wanted to get it out of the way. Not that it's any business of yours.'

'But why have you brought it in that box? We're supposed to hand it in in these folders Miss gave us,' I said, relishing the opportunity to correct Ruth. She started to unload the box.

'My mother said that the museum could borrow some of the things my great-grandad picked up in Italy — for the display. Like these lovely watercolour paintings he bought in Rome — and this beautiful music box . . .'

'Where's the detonator?' I asked, interrupting Ruth's flow.

'It's in the fire brigade museum!' Esme said, breaking into a raucous laugh.

Ruth looked at us in such a superior way and then started to pack away the paintings and the music box. 'For your information the detonator is at the Ministry of Defence!' With that, she pushed us aside and walked haughtily out of the room, shouting back at us:

'I'm going to find somewhere safe to store my project. I don't trust you two!'

Esme and I laughed. I didn't feel like laughing. There was something about the way Ruth had said, 'I don't trust you two.' It was as if she was blaming me for what my grandad had done.

'Well?' Esme said, breaking into my thoughts. 'At least you know now. Your grandad didn't know anything about the concentration camps. Remember what Dominic was saying?'

'Yes,' I said, although I was miles away.

'Saves us another trip to the library. Saves us getting nagged by that awful librarian.'

'I've still got loads to do, though. Lots more questions to ask my grandad and things to find out,' I said, thinking aloud. I felt weighed down with all that I had to do.

'Yes – but at least now you know that your grandad definitely wasn't a traitor,' Esme said quietly.

'You're right, Esme. He wasn't!' I said, slightly more cheered.

'So it's Dominic that's wrong. You just tell him, Claire. Tell him what Miss Sanders said.'

'Dominic doesn't listen,' I said, thinking aloud again.

The words of Dominic's threat seemed to roll around my head: 'You're in trouble when Dad finds out what you've been saying, saying, saying . . .'

'Don't say anything, Dominic,' I said under my breath. 'Let me finish it first, please.'

'What?' Esme asked, half smiling.

87

'I was just – sort of wishing aloud, Esme.'

'Oh,' she said, still confused. 'What about?'

'I hope Dominic doesn't say anything to Mum and Dad before I've found out all of Grandad's story. Or – I don't know what they'll say and then I won't be able to finish my project.'

'Just tell Dominic to keep his big trap shut,' Esme said, forcefully. 'I would if I was you.'

If only it was that easy.

16

On Saturday it was cold and miserable. I didn't feel like getting out of my warm, weekend bed, let alone going to Grandad's. Then I remembered Miss Sanders's threatening words and like an alarm clock they propelled me quickly from under the duvet. The rest of the house was silent.

'We'll have a lazy day tomorrow,' Mum had said on Friday night.

'Yes,' Dad had agreed. 'No football this weekend so we can have a good lie-in.'

'And a do-nothing day. We all need a break,' Mum said. Chris stretched out and smiled at the prospect of a lazy weekend. Dominic lay across the floor, his eyes fixed firmly on the courageous deeds of the hero whose face filled the television screen.

'I need to go to Grandad's, Mum, to finish this project,' I half-whispered.

'Fine,' my mum said, her tone becoming more clipped and businesslike. 'You'll have to get your own breakfast, though.'

'And don't disturb the rest of us,' Dominic grunted without turning round.

*

'It has to be handed in next Friday, Grandad,' I said as soon as Grandad opened the door. He was wearing a blanket around his shoulders and he stooped towards me as he held the door back. 'So can we get down to it quickly, you know, try and get it finished?'

'Good morning, Claire – and how are you this rotten morning?' Grandad asked, forcing a smile. The back room was boiling and foggy, as if Grandad had already smoked a packet of Woodbines. He quickly made me a hot chocolate and placed two fig rolls on the edge of my armchair.

'I've an awful cold, Claire. Sure, honest to God, I feel like I'm dying,' Grandad said, as he emptied his tea cup and fiddled around searching for a Woodbine.

'Sorry, Grandad,' I said, feeling guilty about my impatience. 'You shouldn't be smoking if you're bad.' Grandad laughed and then coughed for several minutes.

'What was it like, Grandad?' I asked.

'How do you mean, Claire?'

'In prison. What was it like?'

'Sure, God knows, you don't waste any time, do you?'

'No – I've got to get it finished and I'm getting worried now.'

Grandad paused for ages, all the time looking into the fire. 'Grandad,' I reminded him. 'What was it like?'

'It's hard to remember it all. Maybe it's because I don't want to remember. Let me see now . . .' He paused for a few minutes again. Then he cleared his throat. 'You know, Claire, after the court we were placed in a big black van. All the other men who didn't

90

turn up for their medical were either Jehovah's Witnesses or Quakers. They were all good men. When we arrived at the prison, an enormous gate opened, then another. It was almost dark. It was December time – not long before Christmas.'

'Were you in prison for Christmas?' I asked, appalled at the thought of Grandad eating his turkey in a prison cell.

'Wait now and I'll tell you,' Grandad said as he moved closer to the fire. 'It was freezing in there, and there were no electric lights like you have today – just gas lamps. So, we were marched up to a desk . . . it was a big wooden thing, a bit like the old pulpits you used to see. Anyway, this prison officer asked you your name and your religion and all sorts of things like that.'

'Were you frightened, Grandad?'

'I was. These men, the officers, they sort of barked at you. If you didn't call them "Sir" there was big trouble. They hated the likes of me – ones who wouldn't fight.'

'So what did you do after you told them your name and all that?'

'Well now . . . I had a bath – just in case I had nits. They took all my clothes and money and put them in a bag until I was released from prison. You know, when I was in the bath, Claire, one of the officers stood there just so I'd wash myself properly – and with the most foul soap!'

'That's horrible, Grandad.'

'Ah, I suppose they had a job to do,' Grandad

sighed. 'Isn't it a strange thing, Claire, a while back I couldn't remember any of this. Now it's all coming back to me. Do you want any more hot chocolate, Claire?'

'No, Grandad,' I said impatiently. 'I just want to hear the rest of your story.'

'Well . . . we were given a set of clothing and then a few bits for the cell – sheets, and things for eating . . .'

'Did you try to escape, Grandad?'

'I did not.' Grandad laughed at my question. Then his whole body shook as he coughed several times.

'What was your cell like, Grandad?' I asked, when he'd finished coughing.

'Ah sure, there was just a dull, old, grey paint over the bare bricks. At the far end of the cell I remember the small window. I used to stand under the window and think how far I was from home. Then I'd sit back on the old, lumpy bed and my heart'd be near breaking with homesickness. Jeez, it was an awful time.'

Grandad turned back to look at the gas fire. He studied the orange columns so closely, as if he was searching for something there. I returned to the row of boxes I was doodling on my notepad and waited for Grandad to start talking again.

The next time I looked, Grandad had drawn the blanket tighter around him and he had fallen asleep. His mouth fell open as he snored gently.

'What about – ?' I began to ask. Grandad's snores grew deeper and slightly louder. 'Grandad,' I said gently.

'What?' he didn't even open his eyes.

92

'Can you tell me any more, please?' I waited for ages for his response.

'Leave it for today, Claire. I think I've a dose of the flu,' he said, his eyes still closed.

'Who will look after you?'

'Roddy'll be here later on,' Grandad said, looking at me now through half-open eyes. 'He'll make me a whisky toddy – sure that's a great cure.'

'But what about – '

'Leave it now, Claire – until Monday, like a good girl.' With that, Grandad closed his eyes again and almost immediately started snoring.

I closed Grandad's front door quietly behind me.

17

Esme insisted on coming with me to see Grandad on Monday. 'All right, but I'm not missing any lessons, so we'll go after school,' I told her sternly.

'Don't be so ratty!' Esme said. So we walked alongside Owlton Park together. There was a biting wind which blew into the stomach of each tree, forcing it to swoop and bend low over the park railings. The mobile park keeper drew a chain around one of the gates ready to padlock them shut. A woman ran towards the gate shouting, 'Oy!' at the keeper. 'Don't lock them yet.' A small child with his scooter ran behind her, battling against the wind.

Roddy answered the door and showed us through into the back room. Grandad's chair was empty. 'He's gone back to bed, Claire,' Roddy said, as if he had spotted the question on my mind. 'To tell you the truth, he's not too good at all.'

Roddy didn't say much more. After a few minutes he brought in two cups of hot chocolate from the kitchen. The room was too warm. It seemed as though the gas fire was glowing from the whole of one wall. Even so, Esme kept her coat on. She sat on the edge of the chair, as if she didn't want to stay long. I felt as though she was looking too closely at Grandad's pictures and photographs.

'How's your project going, Claire?' Roddy asked.

'Not bad. I was hoping to finish it tonight. You see, it has to be handed in on Friday. I was hoping Grandad would tell me the rest . . .' I paused for a moment. 'About the rest of his time in prison.' I felt slightly uneasy talking about this to Roddy. I didn't want to be disloyal.

'Well, to tell you the truth, Claire,' Roddy said quietly, 'I'm not too sure about the rest of his time in prison but I do know what happened to him after he left the place.'

'Tell us! Tell us!' Esme said excitedly.

'You see, I wasn't in the gaol with him so I wouldn't know about that side of things, but he used to talk an awful lot about leaving the prison,' Roddy almost whispered.

'Why?' I asked. 'Wasn't he glad to get out?'

'Wait till you hear. It was a few days before Christmas,' Roddy began. He was sitting beside the fire with his back against the chimney breast. His hands clutched a cup of tea. Esme leaned forward.

'Was he in for Christmas?' Esme asked.

'Now then, I don't want any interruptions whilst I'm telling this or I might lose my place.' Roddy looked solemnly at Esme and me as he spoke. 'Grandad was sentenced to six months' imprisonment or two months' hard labour. He thinks he would have been sent to Dartmoor to break rocks if he'd opted for the hard labour so he chose the prison sentence.

95

What a choice! He was put in the workshop sewing mailbags.'

'Mailbags?' Esme interrupted him.

'Yes, the sort the postman uses to collect your letters. Anyway, all those who were put into the sewing shop had to do eight stitches to the inch – they were checked every so often. So, there's your grandad, in the sewing shop, busily sewing away, when a letter came to the prison governor. It was a very important letter as far as your grandad was concerned.' Roddy stretched his legs out in front of him. The cup of tea was placed carefully on the hearth.

I could sense that Esme was bursting with questions but she had her hand over her mouth as she leaned forward, as if to silence herself.

'The letter was from the manager of a coal-mine in Leicestershire. It said that there was a job there for your grandad as soon as he was "available" to accept it. Now the one thing that you have to remember, Claire and Esme, is that coal-mining was an essential industry during the war. That meant that if you were working in the pits, you didn't have to join the armed forces. A lot of the miners wanted to fight for their country so their jobs were vacant. I was already working there so I asked my boss to sort out a job for your grandad. Back in Lincoln, himself was called to the governor and told that he was being released so that he could work in the pits.'

'So that's how he escaped?' I asked.

'Yes, it was a sort of escape, wasn't it?' Roddy said thoughtfully. 'It wasn't that easy though, and for all sorts of reasons nobody came to meet your grandad from prison. He had had very little money when he went into prison so he was destitute when he was released.'

'What does that mean?' Esme asked cautiously.

'It means he had nowhere to live and no money. He told the governor. He asked a charity who helped out poor prisoners if they'd give your grandad some money. The only thing was, they weren't too happy about helping men who had refused to fight. So they didn't give him anything.'

'So what happened to him?' I asked, nervous about interrupting Roddy.

'He was released from prison early one Friday morning with a few shillings in his pocket. If he'd robbed a bank or attacked someone or married two women at the same time, he would have been given money. As it was, he had refused to fight and during the war that was a worse crime than any.

'He set off walking from Lincoln prison. He didn't realize that, if he had asked, the prison governor would have given him a train pass to reach Leicester. The governor didn't know where your grandad was going so he didn't offer him a pass. So, he walked for a day. In the evening he came to a hostel run by the Angels' Brigade, a very old charity. Your grandad asked them if he could have a bed for the night. They wanted to know why he was homeless so he told them the truth. "No cowards will sleep under this roof!" they told your grandad. He was amazed – but in their eyes he had committed a terrible sin.'

'So, for two nights in the freezing December weather, your grandad slept rough.'

'Whereabouts did he sleep?' I asked.

'I'm not sure. All I know is this: years ago, they used to come around collecting just before Christmas for the Angels' Brigade. They had a band. They stood at the top of each street and they played carols. The kids used to ask for money to put in their tins but your grandad wouldn't let them have any money. "That shower turned me away at my weakest hour. I wouldn't give them the itch!" He used to say that so bitterly every Christmas.'

Roddy stopped talking and looked into the dregs of his tea. Esme leaned back in her armchair again and watched the orange columns of the gas fire. I closed my eyes and tried to imagine what it would be like sleeping outside in the freezing cold December wind. How did Grandad manage without a duvet or a blanket? What if he didn't have his coat with him?

The silence was broken by two loud knocks on the ceiling. 'That's your grandad,' Roddy said, standing up quickly.

'We've been here ages, Claire,' Esme almost whispered. 'Do you think we ought to be going?'

I wanted to see Grandad before I went home. I wanted to see if he was all right after having to sleep out on a December night. Then I remembered that it was over fifty years ago.

'Claire, I'd better be going home,' Esme spoke a bit louder this time.

'Oh . . . oh, all right. Do you want me to walk up to

98

the end of the road with you?' Grandad's road is a bit dark and frightening on winter evenings. The bare trees form eerie shadows below the street lights.

Roddy bustled into the room before Esme had a chance to reply. 'Girls, I'm sorry about this. I'll have to ring the doctor and ask him to come out again. Your grandad's not looking too good.'

'Will he be all right?'

'Yes. I don't think these tablets are any use to him though. Now, will you see yourselves out? I'll have to sort things out before the doctor comes.'

Esme and I walked along to the end of the road. It was so dark – one of the street lights had failed and there seemed to be dark figures looming behind every hedge.

'It's a bit spooky down here, isn't it?' Esme said.

'I know.' I couldn't stop thinking about Grandad. He had been so brave – people had been cruel to him by denying him money and a place to sleep. He had been through such an awful time.

When people are a long way from home and they've got nowhere to sleep for the night – what happens if they get the flu? What if Grandad had caught the flu as he walked along the road from Lincoln prison? He wouldn't have been able to ring the doctor and ask him to call around.

It was such a cold, windy evening. I couldn't wait to get home into the warm.

18

It wasn't warm and cosy at home.

'You'll never guess what,' Chris said in his usual gossipy manner. 'Dominic's been fighting with Jack Davies!' Ruth's brother. The icy-cold feeling returned to my stomach.

'Hello, Claire,' Mum wandered into the hall. 'Can you tell me why boys fight?' She was furiously brushing dried mud off Dominic's coat. 'Had a good day?'

'He won though,' Chris continued, as if ignoring Mum's important question.

'He won, Chris? His trousers are ripped, his shirt is beyond repair, his lovely new coat is filthy and he's got a great gash across his face along with a black eye. How is that winning, hey? Tell me.'

'You should see Jack Davies, Mum,' Chris said, almost laughing.

'And why Jack Davies? I thought they were friends. It isn't funny, Chris. It isn't funny at all,' Mum said, reproaching Chris for his smile.

I knew why it was Jack Davies, even though I couldn't say it to Mum. How could I begin to explain about Jack's great-grandad being a hero and our grandad being . . . well, what was he? 'Any tea, Mum?' I asked quietly.

'Yes, love, I saved you some. I'm glad you didn't eat at your grandad's – all those fries he cooks. They're no good for you.'

'He's ill,' I said, lifting the hot plate from the oven.

'I'm not surprised,' Mum said unsympathetically. 'The lifestyle he leads.'

'Roddy's looking after him. He was just ringing the doctor when we left – the tablets are making him worse.'

'Well, he ought to cut back on the fags and the drink and the fried food. I don't have much sympathy for your grandad, Claire, because he's been told that many times by the doctors to change his lifestyle and he takes absolutely no notice of them.'

'I can't get any sense out of him,' Dad said as he bustled into the kitchen. 'What are you going to do about that temper of his?'

'How do you mean?' Mum asked, breaking off again from brushing Dominic's coat. Chris sat huddled over the table to one side of me and pinched a chip from my plate. I wasn't bothered – I didn't feel all that hungry. Chris sat chewing, enjoying the drama unfolding before him.

'He said that Jack Davies insulted our family – he's been at him for a few days and Dominic reckons he just snapped.'

'Well, what exactly did Jack say that was so dreadful?' Mum asked anxiously.

'Oh, I can't work it out – something like, "You're a

bunch of Irish traitors." Do you know what it was, Chris?'

'Something like that,' Chris said, nudging me.

'Well, that's nonsense. Fancy fighting over that,' Mum said, almost sighing with relief. 'I mean, we're not even Irish! Honestly, why does Dominic have to be so – '

'We're partly Irish,' I said quietly. 'Grandad's Irish, so that makes us – '

'Yes, Dominic says that you know the whole story, Claire,' Dad said, turning towards me purposefully.

'Me?' the chips were slowly disappearing from my plate as Chris munched away as though he was eating popcorn at the cinema. 'Me? I didn't even see the fight, it's nothing to do with me.' Panic was forcing my voice upwards.

'Chips seem to taste nicer a few hours after they've first been cooked – provided they've been kept warm,' Chris said, closely examining one of my chips.

'Oh, for goodness' sake, Chris!' Mum snapped, finally losing patience and banging the clothes-brush down on the kitchen table. 'We're trying to find out why Dominic got into this stupid fight and all you can do is eat your sister's dinner and philosophize about chips! Please tell us – what exactly happened?'

'I've told you once,' Chris said, now more animated.

'Is it all right if I go upstairs, Mum? I've got loads of homework,' I asked hopefully.

'Let's leave it for tonight, Linda,' Dad said gently. 'We're all getting into a bit of a state about something that's . . . well, it's not a great deal, is it? I mean, it's only a fight.'

'Sean, that boy almost hospitalized Dominic. Before we go up to school, all guns blazing, I want to know exactly what happened.'

'Can I?' I asked again. Lead fell to the pit of my stomach as I heard Mum mention going up to the school.

'Yes, go, love,' Mum said. She looked tired and exasperated.

Dominic had one eye covered with a dripping bag of frozen peas. The gash on his face was only a scratch. 'I'm sorry about your fight,' I said hesitantly.

'So you should be. It's all your fault – you started those stupid stories. I hope you've told Mum and Dad.'

'They're not stories, Dominic. It's true. I found out more this evening and when you read Grandad's story you'll – '

'Oh, get lost,' Dominic interrupted. 'You're giving me even more of a headache.'

'What did you have to fight about it for?'

'You wouldn't understand, Claire. You couldn't care less about your family – if you did you wouldn't spread those stupid stories. Do you know what Ruth Davies has been saying? Do you?'

'It's not worth fighting about, Dominic.'

'Go away. You're getting on my nerves.'

In my bedroom, away from the shouting and the black

eyes, I wrote up the last part of Grandad's story. 'Tomorrow,' I thought, 'I'll explain to Mum and Dad. I'll let them read the whole story and then they'll understand. Tomorrow – when it's all finished and neat and ready to be handed in.' They might be a little bit shocked but they wouldn't react like Dominic.

At the front of the project I stuck the photo Grandad had given me of him and Roddy. Underneath I wrote, 'My Grandad's Story'.

Dad wasn't at breakfast on Tuesday morning. 'He's gone to the hospital,' Mum said as she buttered bread for sandwiches. 'Your grandad's been taken seriously ill.'

19

Ruth's voice trailed along the corridor, so loud and self-righteous, interrupting my thoughts about Grandad. 'At first they were talking about going to the police.'

'The police?' Jamie interrupted. 'What for?'

'About the fight – but now they've decided to sort it out through the school. My dad says, "What can you expect with a grandad like that?"' That's when I knew exactly what she was talking about. I had just walked into the room and a sudden silence fell like the curtain at the end of a play.

'It's only a fight,' Jamie said. He sat snugly at his desk and barely turned his head to address Ruth. Esme sat on the edge of her desk, looking towards the crowd who'd gathered for the post-mortem on the fight. Now that I was in the room they weren't talking so freely.

'Grandad's in hospital,' I whispered to Esme. 'He's very bad. Don't tell anyone, will you?'

'What's up with him?'

'I'm not sure, but Dad's been with him during the night.'

During registration I couldn't stop thinking about

Grandad sitting in the boiling-hot back room with a blanket around his shoulders, coughing into the gas fire. Miss Sanders was giving us exact details about how our projects were to be handed in.

'I must say,' she continued. 'Ruth presented her project a week ahead of the deadline and what an achievement!' The class turned and craned their necks to look at Ruth. I couldn't be bothered – I already hated the smug smile that was probably plastered across her face. 'Now Ruth has included some paintings and ornaments brought back from Italy by her great-grandfather. The museum have said that they'll be pleased to display anything like this. But – and it's a very big but – make sure you label your belongings. Any questions?'

'My mum wants to know when the exhibition begins, Miss,' Jamie asked.

'It starts on January the second – just after Christmas. There's a bit of a gap as they have to collate all the material and display it in a way that people will want to see it.'

'Is it all right to type your work on the computer, Miss? You know, to make it neater?' Ruth asked.

'Why are you asking, Ruth?' I snapped. 'You've already handed yours in, so what difference does it make to you?' People began to snigger. I heard Jamie whisper, 'Yes!'

'Claire!' Miss Sanders shouted. 'That's quite enough of that.'

I'd had quite enough of Ruth. She was annoying me so much. 'You just try to make people feel small so

106

that your story will seem like the best one in the world!' Esme tugged my arm as if to quieten me.

'Stop it, Claire. There's no need for that!' Miss Sanders shouted again.

'I was only trying to help,' Ruth said, like an injured puppy, in the most sickly-sweet voice. Then in a harsher tone, 'I won't bother any more.'

'If you want to,' Miss Sanders pronounced each word carefully, 'You can use a word processor or typewriter to present your work. It does make it easy to read.'

I'd already lost interest in the argument with Ruth. I wanted the day to end so that I could find out what was wrong with Grandad. As we filed out of the room Miss Sanders reached out a restraining arm towards me. 'Wait!'

Esme and I wandered over to the window to wait for Miss Sanders. I pressed my nose against the cold pane and looked out across the deserted playing-fields. A car was driving towards the front of the school. My head involuntarily jerked back from the window in recognition. It was Mum and Dad. I could just see Dominic sitting in the back. 'Here they come, Esme,' I whispered. 'All guns blazing.'

20

'I know how you feel,' Esme said comfortingly as we walked home from school together. 'I felt awful when my mum was in hospital – I felt so lost and lonely without her.'

I wished that we could go to Grandad's and tell him about the day. Tell him about Miss Sanders lecturing me and saying how she'd noticed a big change in me just recently. Then she'd become all sympathetic and asked if everything was all right at home because she'd heard that Dominic had been in a fight yesterday. I so longed to sit in Grandad's back room with a cup of hot chocolate and a piece of flapjack. Just me and Grandad, Woodbine smoke gradually filling the room, talking about how ridiculous school and teachers can be.

'What was wrong with her?'

'Who?' Esme asked, surprised.

'Your mum when she was in hospital. What was up with her?'

'She was having my little sister.'

'Oh, Esme, that's not the same! Grandad's seriously ill!'

'I know, I know. I was just trying to help. It doesn't

matter what's wrong – it still feels the same if one of your family is in hospital.'

I couldn't be bothered arguing with Esme. It seemed a bit petty to be saying that my grandad was far worse than her mum.

Dad was sitting at the kitchen table, his hands wrapped around a mug, staring out at the windy garden. I thought something awful had happened at first. He was so still.

'Is it Grandad?' I asked.

'What?'

'Is Grandad – '

'He's a lot better actually, Claire,' Dad said, as if he was waking from a dream. 'They've changed his antibiotics and encouraged him to eat properly and it's amazing how he's rallied. He'll probably be home by the weekend. Good day at school?'

'Not bad. I've loads of homework to do.'

'This project?'

'Yes. It has to be written up in neat. I want to try and finish it this evening and hand it in tomorrow.'

'You've worked so hard on it, Claire – what with all the research and all the time you've spent interviewing Grandad.'

'I know. It's been brilliant doing it,' I said, my thoughts elsewhere.

'Will you let your mum and me read it before you hand it in?' Dad looked closely at my face, checking my expression for an answer before I spoke. He used to look at me like this when I was small and he knew

109

I'd done something wrong and he wanted to see if I would answer honestly.

'Yes,' I said hesitantly. 'Why?'

'Well, if it's going to be on display in a museum we want to make sure there are no spelling mistakes, don't we? We had a quick word with Miss Sanders this morning,' Dad said without a pause.

'Did you? I saw you driving into school.'

'Yes. She said your project is shaping up very well. That's another reason I want to have a good look at it.'

'What about Dominic?'

'It's all sorted now. Jack's mum and dad aren't too happy but it's best the lads shake hands and forget about it. Fights happen at school.' Dad gazed out of the window again for a few minutes. 'Do you want to see your grandad tomorrow?'

'In hospital? Yes please, Dad.'

'Right, we'll sort something out. Perhaps we could go at lunchtime? Now, what shall we do for tea?'

Later on, I checked through my project. I was so, so proud of my story about Grandad. I kept spreading it out across my bed, admiring the neat handwriting and decorated chapter headings. Then I gathered all the sheets together and placed them carefully into the folder that Miss Sanders had given us weeks before. I've never been all that brilliant at school and I felt as though Grandad's story was like a turning point – as though from now on I'd be cleverer.

Grandad didn't have any souvenirs from the war –

apart from his driving licence and identity card. The photograph on the identity card showed a young man with curly hair, smiling cheekily at the camera. It seemed funny seeing Grandad with hair, even though the smile hadn't changed.

With the driving licence and identity card stuck carefully to a piece of paper, my project was ready. Then Esme rang. Nothing too important – she wanted to know if she still had to use paragraphs if she wrote her grandad's story on the computer.

It wasn't a typical Esme phone call where she stays on for ages and gossips about everyone in the class. She was rushing, she said, to finish her project.

Mine was finished and I felt so relieved – like it was the end of term. 'Can I have a look?' Mum asked as I replaced the receiver. 'Just to check there's no big mistakes.'

'Yes, Mum.' I suddenly began to feel slightly anxious. 'What will she think of Grandad now?' I thought. But there was no way out – Mum and Dad always liked to check my work before I handed it in. 'Anyway,' I said to myself, 'they have to find out some time.'

My project was no longer on the edge of the table in my room. I ran down to see if I'd left it beside the phone. It wasn't there. At first I wasn't worried – I thought I had put it down somewhere and forgotten I'd left it there. I was always doing things like that. I searched my room, then the lounge, where Mum and Dad were watching a programme about the Antarctic.

The whiteness filling the screen made me shiver. No sign of it anywhere. 'I must have put it in my bag,' I said, half to myself.

It wasn't there. 'Have you seen my folder?' I asked Chris as he chased a computer monster across the screen.

'No,' he said, distracted. 'Ask Dominic.'

'Have you seen my folder?' Even though his bruised eye was half closed I knew as soon as I'd asked him. 'Dominic,' I asked again, 'have you seen it?'

'Yes.'

'Where is it then? Mum wants to have a look at it.'

'I've hidden it.'

'What? You've no right. Give it back now! I have to hand it in tomorrow.'

'No!'

'Dominic, you're not funny. Just give it back.'

'I said no – now get out of my room!'

'Don't be so nasty, Dominic. It isn't even your property.' I tried to sound as official and controlled as Dominic, but the anger was making me tearful.

'What's going on?' Mum appeared in the doorway. I ran down the stairs. 'Dominic,' she asked again, 'what have you done to Claire?'

21

'You tell them, Claire,' Dominic hissed. His voice was filled with menace. 'Tell them why I've hidden your thing about our grandad.'

'I don't know,' I whispered through my tears. This was so unfair. Grandad's story was the best work I'd ever done in my life and Dominic had taken it away from me, saying I couldn't hand it in.

Mum had insisted that Dominic come downstairs and sort the matter out. Dad had reluctantly turned off the Antarctic. Chris came down and sat curled up at the end of the settee, like he was watching a slightly frightening film.

This wasn't how I wanted Mum and Dad to read Grandad's story. I'd found out about Grandad, not Dominic – yet here was Dominic shouting, like an angry dog barking at stray rubbish being blown by the wind. It was the best thing I'd ever done and Dominic was ruining it. I hated Dominic so much that I felt as though I wanted to hit the other side of his face so that both eyes would be bruised.

'It's either full of lies or if it's true it shouldn't be on show in the museum!' Dominic said angrily.

'You don't know what you're talking about,

113

Dominic,' I said, my throat sore from the tears. 'You haven't heard the whole story. You don't really know the truth about Grandad.'

'What are you two on about?' Dad said, annoyed that his evening peace had been ruined.

'You read it and see,' Dominic sneered, pulling my precious folder from under a settee cushion and throwing it at Dad. 'You'll see that Grandad went to prison during the war. I'm not proud of that and I don't see why we should all have to suffer just because it makes a good story for Claire's stupid project.'

'What?' Mum asked, disbelieving.

'You read it, Mum, and see what Grandad was like.'

'Dominic, you don't know anything about Grandad!' I shouted.

'Dominic, you're getting to be a right drama queen,' Dad said in a resigned voice. He walked over and switched the television back on. 'Give Claire her project and let's settle down again.'

'Hang on a minute, can we sort this out?' Mum looked puzzled and slightly in pain. 'I can't concentrate with that thing on, love.' Her hands were gently clutching the side of her face.

'I hate you, Dominic,' I snarled.

'Claire, what's this all about?' Mum asked quietly, her eyes closed as if the whole room was giving her a headache.

'It's Dominic, he's trying to bully me – because of Grandad's story.'

'But why? Why are you like this so suddenly? Dominic, answer me!' Mum's voice rose slightly.

114

'Mum, you've got to read this thing Claire has done for history – then you'll see what I'm on about.'

'Oh, for goodness' sake, Dominic! It's only a history project. What is the matter with you?' Dad shouted. 'Linda, why don't you let them sort it out themselves. I've had a really tough day at work. I can do without all this.'

'Sorry, Dad, but it's not my fault,' I said.

'Dominic, get back upstairs,' Mum said firmly, 'and please quit the amateur dramatics! Claire, you stay here with your dad. I'm going to sit quietly in the kitchen and read this project.'

'Can I read it after you, Mum?' Chris asked, as if it was a weekly comic that we were all dying to read. Mum ignored him.

I sat beside Dad and waited patiently.

'Tomorrow, Claire, I'm taking some things in to Grandad. We'll have to go to the house first and then to the hospital. Do you want to come? It'd be nice to see Grandad again, wouldn't it?'

'Yes. What about Chris and Dominic?'

'They can go another time. I know you're anxious to see him.'

'Have you read this? Did you know this about your father?' Mum burst back into the room. 'Read it!' She placed the folder very firmly into Dad's hands.

'What . . . what is it about?' Dad asked, puzzled.

'It's your father's war record!' She pronounced each word carefully and clearly. 'Claire has written it for her project – the one they are going to display in the museum.'

'What about it?' Dad asked, glancing back at the television.

'Sean, I cannot believe that you don't know anything about what happened to your father during the war.'

'I don't,' Dad said, as if Mum had accused him of lying.

'What's wrong, Mum?' I asked quietly. She didn't answer me, she just continued to glare at Dad.

'Part of me isn't at all surprised, knowing what your father is like – but another part of me is shocked. I would never have believed it!'

'Linda, honestly, I don't know what you're on about.'

'Read it,' Mum said sternly, tapping my project again. 'Read it and see!'

22

I sat on the top stair, trying hard to hear what Mum and Dad were saying. My dressing-gown was wrapped tightly around me against the chill, even though it wasn't a cold night and the heating was on full blast. The computer beeped every few seconds in Chris's room and Dominic played a slow, depressing tape – probably about a fifteen-year-old boy with spots.

'Go to your room, Claire,' Mum had snapped half an hour earlier. 'Get ready for bed.'

'What about Grandad's story?'

'Claire, do as you're told,' Mum snapped again.

'Why? I haven't done anything wrong.'

'Claire.' Mum's tone softened. She massaged her forehead, drawing her hair back from her face. 'Please, Claire. Your dad and I need some time to discuss a few things. Off you go now, like a good girl.'

Chris joined me on the top stair. 'What gets me,' he whispered urgently, 'is that when they're in a bad mood and "need to talk", we get sent to our rooms.'

'Yes,' I said vaguely.

'Why can't they go to their room? We all get sent upstairs, nobody can watch the telly or make toast or do anything downstairs, just so they can talk. They're dead selfish.'

'Just listen, Chris!'

'What's so special about that room? Why do they always have to have their "talks" in that room? Makes me sick.'

'Shut up, Chris, and listen! I can't hear what they're saying. I'm in dead trouble if I don't hand in that project.'

Dad's voice was raised in protest. 'You can't do that, Linda. She's worked so hard on it these last few weeks.' Mum hissed a reply.

'What did she say?' Chris asked. It wasn't real life for him – just another drama he was watching.

'I didn't know anything about it – I'm as surprised as you are!' Dad shouted. Another subdued reply from Mum, then Dad again. 'No! that's totally unfair. You haven't read it properly, you've just skimmed through it looking for the bad parts. I know you were never keen on my father but there's no need to take your prejudice this far!'

'We'd better make ourselves scarce,' Chris whispered. 'I think she's about to make an exit.' At that moment the lounge door was pulled open quickly. I had only just closed my bedroom door when I heard Mum running up the stairs. The whole house seemed to shake for ages after she slammed her door. I didn't hear Dad going upstairs. I must have fallen asleep.

'Where's your project?' Esme asked as we waited for the usual late arrival of Miss Sanders. 'I thought you'd finished it – you said you were going to hand it in today.'

'I've forgotten it. It was on the cupboard, next to my bag and I forgot to pack it.' I wasn't talking to a teacher and it wasn't an original story. It was too painful to explain.

It can be really funny listening to people saying why they haven't brought their homework into school:

'The dog got it.'

'My little sister chewed it.'

'I've left it on the desk in my room. I can see it now, Miss. Honest.'

'I've done it in rough, I just need to copy it up.'

'I left it on the bus, I was showing it to someone.'

'It's been stolen. Our house was burgled.'

Esme prattled on about her project – how she was going to do this and that before she eventually handed it in on Friday. I sat and thought carefully about which excuse I would use. In my mind I imagined myself choosing my excuse carefully, like selecting a book from a library shelf.

'Where's my project, Mum?' I had asked at breakfast. She looked as though she hadn't slept. Her normally immaculate make-up was smudged. 'I want to hand it in today, get it out of the way. Where is it? Can I have it back, please?'

'No.' She didn't look at me. She watched the marmalade glisten on her toast before lifting it to her mouth.

Dominic said, 'Good for you, Mum,' then he scraped his chair back noisily before leaving the kitchen.

'I wish Dominic would learn to clear his plate from the table before leaving the room. He was born into the wrong class and the wrong age, you know. Needs servants.'

'Why not?' I asked. I clenched my fists, longing to be reasonable and calm. Chris collected Dominic's plate before taking his own over to the sink. He stood, arms deep in warm, soapy water, wiping and wiping and wiping. And listening.

Mum spooned another blob of marmalade on to her second piece of toast and smoothed it meticulously to each corner of the slice. 'Because,' she said slowly and thoughtfully, 'because I don't want you to – no, that's not right – I don't think that you *should* hand it in.'

'Why not?' Clenching my fists even tighter.

'I'll write you a note for Miss Sanders. I'm sure she'll understand.'

'Why not?' I asked again. 'Why won't you tell me?'

'Oh, don't cry, Claire, for goodness' sake. Your eyes will be all red and sore when you arrive at school and they'll think . . . Look, it isn't the end of the world.'

'Linda!' Dad shouted from the front door, 'Do you want a lift this morning? I'm going now, this minute.'

'No.'

'No, thank you,' I wanted to correct her. The front door slammed without a goodbye. Mum shivered.

'Why not, Mum?'

'Oh God, Claire, you look so pitiful. Darling, it isn't your fault – it'll take me ages to explain now so it's best that we leave it till this evening. Chris, are you washing those plates or redesigning the pattern on them? Come on, let's get ready for the day.'

'Please, Mum, please let me hand it in.'

'No, love. Let's leave it for now. It's time to get ready, Claire.'

I still couldn't think of a good excuse. It seemed almost too childish to say, 'My mum won't let me hand it in.' I couldn't believe it – after all my hard work. What excuse could I possibly use?

23

Grandad's house smelt like a morning pub – all stale smoke and beer dregs. Dad was upstairs sorting out some clean clothes for Grandad before we went to the hospital. I sat on the stool in Grandad's kitchen, my eyes fixed on the broken fridge magnet. 'Chica' was at the top and 'go' had fallen to the very bottom of the fridge door. I suppose it had always been like that but I'd never really noticed it before. Normally Grandad stood in front of it, mixing hot chocolate or turning over sausages. 'Chica – go'. It sounded more like a message than a city in America.

I'll tell Grandad! The idea came to me suddenly as I gazed at where Grandad should have stood. I'll tell him about Mum and he'll go mad and insist that Dad finds the project and hands it in. Yes! Grandad would sort things out, I'd seen him do it before.

'Ready, Claire?' Dad asked as he stood at the bottom of the stairs with a small suitcase of Grandad's clothes. The doorbell rang. 'That'll be Roddy.'

'How are ye?' Roddy asked. 'Listen, I've the dinner on over the road so I won't stop – I always have my big meal in the middle of the day. Here's today's *Sporting Life* for himself. Arrah, they don't sell it on the hospital trolleys – well, why would they? Sure there's very little chance of getting to the bookies'. There's a few sweets and a couple of miniatures and, of course, the old Woodbines.'

'Why don't you come with us, Roddy?' I'm not sure if it was a genuine invitation from Dad. Sometimes he says things like that when he expects the answer to be no. Roddy thought, as if calculating something, for a few minutes.

'Why don't I, indeed? Listen, I'll nip over and switch off the old bacon and cabbage and I'll be right with you. Sure a free agent can have his dinner any time!'

We waited in the car. I was glad – there seemed to be something more than Grandad missing from the house. It didn't feel right, sitting in Grandad's back room looking at the empty ashtray and Grandad's chair facing the quiet television.

'You seem a bit happier now,' Dad said, as he gazed out over Owlton Park.

'I am. We'll sort it out – about the project. I'm not worried any more.'

'Good – but don't depend on your mother, Claire. She can be a very stubborn woman, you know.' I wasn't listening. Everything would be sorted out.

'Poor old Roddy,' Dad sighed as we watched Roddy walk quickly back from his house. He looked as though he'd developed a limp in his left leg. 'He'd be lost if anything happened to your grandad, you know. Old age, eh? All it seems to promise is loneliness – if you're healthy, you watch your friends dying before you – '

'Nothing will happen to Grandad, Dad. He's getting better, remember?'

At the hospital the ward sister asked to speak to Dad privately. Roddy and I had to sit in a small waiting-room outside the ward.

'Something's up,' Roddy said confidently.

'No, they're just making arrangements for when Grandad can leave hospital.'

'No, there's something wrong. I could tell by the way that nurse spoke to your father.' Roddy looked anxiously beyond the square window in the swing door. 'All the same, I hope to God he's all right.'

'He will be, Roddy. He's supposed to be coming home at the weekend, don't worry.' Although I was trying to reassure Roddy I felt like some reassurance for myself. 'I wonder where Dad is?'

'He was such a brave, courageous man,' Roddy said.

'He's not dead or anything, Roddy.' I felt angry that Grandad should be talked about in the past tense.

'No, no. But when he was younger, I meant. You know – what we were talking about before, during the war. He was so full of courage.'

I thought for a few minutes about Roddy's words. 'Was he? I still can't understand. I mean, if he was so full of courage, why didn't he fight, Roddy? Why didn't he answer that letter behind the clock?' As soon as I'd spoken I knew I'd said the wrong thing. I felt as though I was betraying Grandad.

Roddy looked annoyed. 'I haven't a clue what you mean.' It wasn't a question – it was as though Roddy wanted to end the conversation. He stood up, walked across the waiting-room and held the door open slightly, as if to overhear what the ward sister might be saying to Dad.

'Why didn't Grandad want to fight?' I asked Roddy. He let the door swing back noiselessly. He sat and thought for ages.

'You know, Claire,' he began to explain, 'we hadn't a clue what was going on. We were young and all we wanted was to earn a bit of money and have a bit of fun. Sure, we had no television to tell us about the war and we had no idea that the Nazis were doing those awful things to the people there. Before we came over to this country we were told "Keep out of that war. Remember, it isn't your war." So, your grandad heeded those words. Do you see?'

'I think so.'

'On top of all that, Claire, a few years before the war, England, well, indeed, Britain – had been at war with Ireland. Honest to God, Claire, for a young one it was so confusing.'

'Was Grandad confused, Roddy?'

'You know,' Roddy said quietly, 'we didn't know who was our friend and who was our enemy – your grandad was never sure if he did the right thing. I know you find it hard, Claire, to understand your poor old grandad. He only did what he thought was right at the time.'

'But why did you say he was brave and courageous?'

'He was, I'm telling you, Claire – he was very brave.'
Roddy stared out through the swing doors again.
'There was one day – working down the pit. I went
down the wrong way and I became trapped. If it
wasn't for your grandad I wouldn't be here today to
tell the story. He helped me – he helped me to escape.
It wasn't easy at all you know, working in the coal-
mines, Claire. It wasn't the easy option that many
thought it was.'

'Is that what you meant . . . do you remember when
we went set dancing? But I thought you saved Grandad's life.'

'All I did was to get the manager of the mine to
write to the governor so that your grandad could be
released, that's all. But your grandad really did save my
life.'

Roddy had just finished speaking when Dad walked
briskly through the swing doors. He fiddled with the
car keys, like he does when he's impatient to set off
somewhere.

'Right, then, show us the way,' Roddy said, picking
up the bag of Woodbines and *Sporting Life*.

'No, not now, Roddy, if you don't mind.'

'Why? Are things not too good?' Roddy asked, shuffling now.

'No, things aren't too good. I've spent some time
with him and he's worn out now. He's wired up to all
sorts – monitoring him.'

'Did they say what . . .' Roddy questioned.

'A stroke,' Dad interrupted. That's all he said – a
stroke. Without speaking he turned and left the room,

walking quickly towards the main exit, jingling the car keys all the time.

'What's a stroke?' I asked Roddy. Dad was ahead of us.

'It's an awful bad dose, Claire. God help your poor grandad. There's few of our age recover from that sort of thing.'

'Will he get better?' Roddy didn't answer. 'Will he get better?' I asked again. I asked a third time. They just looked at one another suspiciously and then opened the front doors of the car.

'What's a stroke?' I asked at the first set of traffic lights.

After a long pause, Dad said, 'I'll explain later. Please be quiet now. Let me concentrate on the driving.'

24

'My great-grandad had a dreadful stroke,' Ruth announced. 'Before he died,' she added with great severity.

'Well, he'd hardly have had one after he died,' Esme whispered.

'I heard that, Esme. Don't be so rude.'

I didn't want all this discussion about Grandad's stroke just after returning from the hospital. I didn't want Ruth to hear, but she's so nosy and she overhears everyone's private conversations.

'He went ga-ga! Had all sorts of flashbacks from his dreadful experiences in the war. Thought he was being attacked by Germans.'

'You said he was in Italy, Ruth,' Jamie interrupted.

'He was. There were Germans in Italy too, you know. Ooh, thick or what?'

'My dad had a stroke,' Jamie said quietly.

'See – it's not such a special thing,' Ruth said, dismissively.

'I wish someone would give you a dreadful stroke!' Esme's comment lightened the atmosphere. Ruth walked away.

'Did he? When did he have it? Is he all right now?' I asked anxiously.

'Not bad. Sometimes he's not able to walk properly and he finds it hard holding things and he gets a bit fed up when he can't say exactly what's on his mind.'

'How does he manage at work?' Esme asked.

'He doesn't go to work any more. He's registered disabled. Mum goes – she works in a delicatessen.'

'What is it? What is a stroke?' I asked Jamie urgently. I had asked Dad again when he dropped me back at school, but he still insisted he'd explain later.

'It's like when something goes wrong on one side of your brain. Mum said it's like when part of the fuse box goes in the electricity. Your brain tells you what to do and if that bit has stopped working – blown a fuse – then you can't do those things any more.'

'Your family don't have much good luck, do they, Jamie? I mean, your grandad got sent away during the war and now this has happened to your dad.'

'No, we don't have much luck,' Jamie agreed. 'He gets physiotherapy, though – and help at a day centre. You can get better, you know.' I was only half-listening to Jamie.

'Shall we go and see your grandad after school?' Esme asked, trying to cheer us up again.

'I don't know. I'm not sure if . . .'

'Go on! We can walk to the hospital. Do you want to come, Jamie?'

'Esme!' I hissed, annoyed. 'You'll be selling tickets next.'

'It's OK,' Jamie said. He looked really hurt. 'I can't go anyway, I have to get home quickly to look after my dad.'

129

'I don't mean to be awful, Jamie,' I said, already regretting what I'd said. 'You can come if you want to. I just don't want ... well, a whole crowd of people going. I mean, imagine if Ruth went – she'd probably be telling the nurses how to do their job.'

'I know the way to the stroke ward,' Jamie said, hopefully, already enthusiastic about the mission.

'What about your dad?' I reminded him.

'Oh, he'll be OK,' Jamie said, dismissively.

It's a long walk from the school to the hospital – especially when you're tired in the late afternoon. Jamie and Esme tried to cheer me up by telling me jokes and talking about people at school but I couldn't smile. It wasn't a trip into town where you get more excited the closer you get to town on the bus.

'You wait here,' I warned Esme and Jamie outside the ward. It was the small side room where Roddy and I had waited earlier in the day.

'Why can't we come with you?' Esme asked, obviously annoyed with me.

'Because it's not right,' I said without thinking. Then: 'Three of us will get stopped but if it's just me they won't notice.' Hospitals are funny like that – hundreds of people walking around and nobody really notices. But three schoolchildren, alone together – they'd stick out.

I left my school bag with Esme and Jamie, held my head up high and walked confidently down the ward, looking for Grandad's bed. 'Hey,' a voice gently called out. I had walked past Grandad. It was Roddy who was calling. 'I decided to come back, Claire.'

I would never have recognized Grandad. He was so pale and lifeless. His right arm and his chest were wired up to a machine that beeped like Chris's computer. 'That must be annoying, Grandad,' I said, without thinking. Grandad smiled. It was a strange, strange smile. Only half of his face moved – the other half remained slumped towards his shoulder.

'I can't wait until Saturday, Grandad, when you're back home. We'll have some flapjack to celebrate, and hot chocolate.'

Grandad slowly opened his mouth. He grunted at me – no words, just grunts. No smiles, just an untidy squiggle.

'What?' I said. 'Talk properly, Grandad!'

His mouth opened again. He looked as though he was underwater at the swimming baths, trying to tell me it was time to go and get changed. 'Grandad!' I said. A dribble of saliva ran from his mouth, across his chin. 'You've got to talk, Grandad. I need you to talk.'

'Go easy, Claire,' Roddy whispered. 'Be gentle with your old grandad.'

'Mum won't let me hand your story in to Miss Sanders. She said it's best if I don't hand it in. I need you to talk, Grandad. Persuade her – tell her she can't do that.'

'He won't be able to do that, Claire,' Roddy said softly.

Grandad opened his mouth slowly and let out a sort of gentle roar. Then he leaned back into the pillow, held at an angle by a type of rack at the top of the bed. He shrugged one shoulder and then he started to cry.

It was awful. It was dreadful. I didn't know what to do. 'Don't, Grandad,' I said firmly. 'Stop it!' The tears trickled down his face, joining forces with the saliva. Roddy leaned over and gently wiped the wetness from Grandad's face. 'What's the matter with you?' I felt so angry with Grandad that I wanted to shake him hard so he'd be able to talk properly and stop blubbering like a baby.

'Roddy, tell Grandad!' Everything in the whole world was different. I had never before seen Grandad cry. Grandads don't cry. They're brave and strong and they put up with everything that people say and do. Nothing seemed to hurt Grandad before. Why was he behaving like this?

'What's up?' the nurse asked. Roddy pointed at me. 'How did you get here? You must have slipped past the desk.' He was smiling.

I couldn't believe that this nurse was being so light-hearted and happy. 'Can't you see my grandad?' I wanted to shout at him. I wanted to get Esme, too, so that she could sort things out.

'Come on,' he said, laughing. 'Say goodbye to your – grandad is it?' He looked over at Roddy for confirmation. Roddy nodded. 'Maybe you could come back later with your parents?'

Grandad's left hand reached out towards me – as if he was saying goodbye.

'When will Grandad be better?' I asked the nurse as

he escorted me out of the ward, humming an annoying tune.

'Your mates are round the corner in that little snack bar. That waiting-room there is for relatives only,' he said, firmly.

'Are you deaf?' I asked, surprising myself. I felt angry with the whole world at that moment. 'I said, "When will Grandad be better?"'

'Don't be so cheeky,' he said, pointing at me, his tone changing. 'Go home and ask your parents. They'll tell you all you need to know.'

25

There was no one at home. The kitchen was cold, stove all clean, no plates warming and no dinner cooking. I felt freezing and my empty stomach made me even more miserable.

In the lounge a note was propped up on the coffee table: 'Claire – gone to hospital. Waited for you! Help yourself to tea or nip round to the chippy.' Next to the note was the morning mail, opened and abandoned. Two bills and a letter from school. I scanned the top of the letter – it was about the Government's league table on truanting. 'Boring!' I shouted to myself.

Back in the kitchen I searched for money for the chippy. No sign – no loose change. Nothing. 'What am I supposed to buy chips with?' I shouted at the neatly closed cupboards. 'Buttons?'

I longed for somebody to be in the house, even if it was Dominic, even if it meant arguing with him.

In the fridge I found some bacon and eggs. I grilled the bacon and scrambled the eggs. The bacon didn't taste half as nice as Grandad's when it was fried. I placed a huge dollop of tomato sauce in the centre of the plate and then savoured every mouthful. 'Bread,' I thought. 'I'll make a big sloppy sandwich. It'll make me feel so much better, like I'm at Grandad's.' Oh, Grandad, Grandad, Grandad.

Mum, Chris and Dominic arrived home at half-past eight. The smell of fish and chips filled the hall and drew me downstairs. 'How's Grandad?' I asked as they rushed to sort out the supper.

'Poor old Grandad,' Dominic said, shaking his head. That made me angry. He didn't mean it.

'Just the same, Claire. I believe you were at the hospital earlier,' Mum said, her voice hardening. 'You shouldn't have done that – children aren't really allowed in at all.'

'Sorry. It was Esme's idea – I was dying to see Grandad. Didn't Dad tell you? I wasn't allowed to see him at lunchtime.'

'You take far too much notice of Esme, Claire,' Mum said.

'Where's Dad?'

'He's staying for a while longer. How was school today?'

'Fine. Mum ... will Grandad get better?' I asked hesitantly. Dominic and Chris were on another planet, impatiently attacking the fish and chips.

'Who knows?' Mum said, shrugging her shoulders.

'Earlier on, while you were at the hospital, Mum, I was thinking ... about the project, you know, "Grandad's Story".'

'Yes.'

'Please, please can I hand it in tomorrow – Thursday, instead of Friday? Being as Grandad's so ill, we can't really sort it out with him.' Dominic stopped

135

eating and looked furiously towards Mum, his shoulders forced back.

'No, Claire,' she said gently. Dominic resumed eating.

'Why not, Mum?' I could feel my mouth quivering and the muscles in my face jumping around.

'I feel dreadful about this, Claire – after you've worked so hard on it and it isn't your fault. It's not a punishment or anything, do you understand?'

'No,' I whispered, breathing deeply to hold back the tears. Dominic and Chris were eating too quietly.

'I feel so strongly about this, Claire.'

'About what, Mum? I don't understand.'

'Well ... how can I put this – nicely, bearing in mind the circumstances?'

'What do you mean?'

'Well, your grandad being so ill. You see, I don't think that the history of this family should be plastered all over a museum. Especially when it's a story that's, well, to be frank, Claire – it's not something we can be proud of, is it?'

'What?'

'No, I agree with you!' Dominic said, his mouth full of food.

'Shut up, fish face!' I hissed.

'Your Grandad refusing to fight. That's not something that I want everyone to know. To be honest, Claire, if he was my dad I'd be ashamed of him. He wasn't even a conscientious objector, he didn't think things through – and if you hand that project in, everyone will know the full details of your grandad's shameful life. I don't want that. I do *not* want that!'

'Good for you, Mum, neither do I!' Dominic said, applauding Mum.

'It wasn't like that, Mum. Grandad didn't know what was happening. He didn't understand.'

'Claire, lots and lots of men and women didn't understand,' Mum said forcefully. 'But they still went and bravely fought and gave their lives for their country.'

'Yeah!' Dominic cheered.

'That's the whole point, Mum. This wasn't Grandad's country,' I said, desperately.

'It doesn't make any difference which was his country, Claire. He should have gone to fight.'

'It does, Mum, it does. He was only eighteen and he was confused, he didn't know what to do. Ask Roddy!'

'He was a traitor, Claire!' Dominic said, forcefully.

'That's enough, Dominic!' Mum snapped. Chris sat watching, finishing the crispy end chips on Mum's plate. I wished he would say something. I so wanted someone to be on my side. 'Anyway, Claire – I'll write a note for Miss Sanders tonight and that'll be the end of the matter. She'll understand.'

'I can't believe it,' I said, gazing out at the black sky. 'I can't believe it. That's the best thing I've ever done in my whole life and it's a brilliant story and you won't let me hand it in. Grandad didn't do anything wrong, you know. He wasn't a traitor – you can't have read it properly, Mum.'

'I know, Claire. You did make a lovely job of it – spelling's great, your handwriting's lovely but you can't hand it in and that's that. And I have read it properly,

Claire,' Mum said firmly. Then in a more gentle voice, 'One day, when you're a bit older, you'll understand.'

How I hated that. 'When you're older you'll understand.' It made me feel as though I was three again and I'd been showing off to a crowd of adults, like you do when you're three. Then you get smacked for being bold and cheeky.

'That's another thing, Claire. The school has contacted me about an unexplained absence last week. Where were you that afternoon? Dentist? I can't remember for the life of me.' Mum was clearing the plates away.

'No,' I said, surly and full of anger. 'I was at the prison!'

26

I handed Mum's letter about the project to Miss Sanders on Thursday morning. It didn't make everything all right. She didn't understand. She was furious.

'What does your mother mean?'

Like Mum the night before.

'The prison? Are you serious?'

Miss Sanders read the letter over and over again.

'I'll have to ring her – this is very worrying, Claire.'

Mum was worried too.

'With Esme? Why? What did you do there? I can't believe this.'

Nor could Miss Sanders.

'It's hard to believe this, Claire.'

I had explained. Exactly. It was a strange feeling but I enjoyed the worried look on Mum's face as I told her about the prison officer answering the door at the front of the prison.

'My God!' Mum had put both hands to her face. 'Did anyone see you – apart from the prison officer? How awful!' She stretched her little fingers out to cover her eyes. 'How could you, Claire?'

'I'll find your mother's work number. We'll have to arrange a meeting – today!' Then Miss Sanders laughed suddenly. 'If everyone did this, there'd be no exhibition. After all the hard work.'

'That settles the matter finally!' said Mum. 'There is no way that you are handing that project in. That is that! No way!'

27

'Linda, for God's sake! I need some support – not all this hassle!' Dad said, his voice full of sadness and fatigue.

'I know, I know, love. I'm trying to be supportive.'

'No, you're not. If you were, you'd just give Claire that blessed project and forget the whole matter. The way that you're carrying on, it seems as though you're trying to punish *me* for what my dad did. Look, I can't cope with it. Not now!' Dad sounded close to tears.

'Love, I'm not trying to punish you,' Mum said gently. 'I'm trying to protect this family from ridicule. It's because I care so much about you and about the children – that's why I'm doing this.'

'Linda, please let it drop. I just can't cope with any problems here. If I'm going to be coming home late every night from the hospital . . . all I want is a bit of peace. Otherwise I think I'll . . . well . . .'

'You'll what?' Mum asked, less sympathetically.

'I feel I'll crack up! My dad is dying – I have to face up to that. It's such a hard thing, you know. Dad needs me to be there with him. That's why I want your support, not all this aggro.'

'Sorry, love,' Mum whispered. I could hardly hear

her. They were sitting in the kitchen. It was one o'clock in the morning. I was on the bottom stair, sitting in my dressing-gown, ready to run up to my room when the chairs scraped back. Dad had only just returned from the hospital.

What did he mean, 'My dad is dying'? Grandad wasn't dying. Jamie's dad didn't die after he'd had a stroke – he had recovered. He has physiotherapy and speech therapy. He's getting better. Grandad will get better too. Why are parents always so bleak and negative? Why do they give up so easily?

I so wanted Grandad to be better – then he'd be able to explain in his own words. If only I could see Grandad and talk to him privately, without Roddy and all the nurses around. I would so love to tell him about Mum's meeting with Miss Sanders.

It was awful.

Miss Sanders had borrowed the Deputy Head's room. The desk was in the corner of the office – paper and books were arranged in neat piles on the desk. A pin-board just above the desk was covered in bits of paper headed, 'Telephone Message'.

In another corner of the room, four cream easy chairs were arranged around a coffee table. There were flowers in the middle of the small table. The Deputy Head's room wasn't like an office – it was more like somebody's sitting-room with the television taken away and a desk pushed into the corner. On the shelves behind the cosy chairs there was a stereo and lots of tapes. I kept thinking how nice it would be to work in this room all day. Much better than a classroom.

Miss Sanders offered Mum an easy chair but Mum refused and said she'd rather sit on an upright one close to the desk. Miss Sanders arranged her papers carefully. I sat on the easy chair. Miss Sanders felt it was better if I was present.

'I think you should know, Miss Sanders, before we start this meeting, that Claire's grandad is in hospital recovering from a stroke.'

'Yes,' Miss Sanders replied coldly. 'Claire did tell me. Now what, exactly, is the problem?' As my grandad would have said: 'Not much love lost between those two.'

'As you know, Miss Sanders, I feel very strongly about this project. Because of what Claire has discovered, I feel that it shouldn't be handed in.'

'Why not?'

'I explained in the letter. I don't want to be going over old ground. I'm not at all happy about pupils writing their family history – I'm sure that plenty of families have skeletons in their cupboards – and I think they should remain there.'

'So you're saying that children shouldn't study history?'

'No, not at all. I think it's good for them to learn about the past – from books and museums – not from their old family secrets,' Mum said firmly.

'Well, we thought – and the Midlands War Memorial Museum thought – that it would be good for children to become historians themselves and find out about a specific period in history.'

'That's fine,' Mum said. 'I have no problem with

that – provided they don't uncover embarrassing . . . stories from their family history.'

'I don't understand what you mean, Mrs Coleman.'

'Well, I'll put it this way: if Claire's grandad had been an ordinary soldier and she'd written about that then I'd have no problem. But he wasn't an ordinary soldier and I don't think his story is anything to be proud of.'

'So, let me get this right, Mrs Coleman – you're saying that we should teach children certain parts of our history?'

'No, I'm not. All I'm saying is that Claire isn't handing in her grandad's story. That's that.' Miss Sanders had made her angry.

'So what's Claire going to say to her classmates when they ask about her project?'

Mum thought for ages. She looked at me as if I would provide an answer. I didn't. I wanted her to be on my side but she wasn't. I looked at Miss Sanders, whose mouth was fixed firmly in a line.

'That's up to Claire,' Mum said. 'She can either tell them the truth or make up her own excuse.'

'And an excellent piece of work goes to waste?' Miss Sanders asked quickly.

'Yes, well, it shouldn't have got this far. Parents should have been informed about this!'

'They were,' Miss Sanders stated triumphantly. Mum fidgeted and looked at her watch.

'I'll have to be going – another appointment,' Mum announced, standing up.

144

'So that's it? You're not going to allow Claire to hand in her work?'

'No,' Mum said finally. 'Now, if you don't mind . . .'

Miss Sanders held the door open for Mum. 'Thank you for your time and concern.' It was like thanking a relation for a present you hated – it was good manners but you didn't mean it.

Miss Sanders walked briskly away from the entrance hall as Mum stopped to kiss me goodbye. 'Oh, by the way, Miss Sanders,' Mum shouted up the corridor. Miss Sanders walked back quickly. 'About Claire's unexplained absence from school last week. Did you know that she'd gone to the prison to do some research for this precious project?' Miss Sanders looked quizzically at my mum. 'No, I didn't think you did. Some things are better left alone.'

If I'd told Grandad all about that meeting, over flapjack and hot chocolate, what would he have said? 'Arrah, Claire, it'll all blow over. You watch, next week when your mum's up to her eyes in work again she'll hand that project over like a lamb.'

She won't, Grandad. There's not time. Today is Friday, deadline day, and I have no story to hand in.

28

I watched the raindrops cling on to the bottom of the washing line and then, when they thought that no one was looking, slowly drip on to the lawn. It was dry now, although it had been raining all night. I had heard every bucketful thrown against my bedroom window while I tried to think of an excuse. I couldn't tell the truth: 'My mum won't let me hand in the project because she's ashamed of my grandad's story.' They might think I was ashamed too. I wasn't. I understood what Grandad had done – even though I still wish he hadn't put the second letter behind the clock.

Dad had left the house early so that he could visit Grandad on his way to work. Mum moved around the kitchen quickly and quietly. Dominic and Chris ate their breakfast in a tired haze. It seemed as though the house was muffled by a blanket of sadness and disappointment.

'I've done a treat for your lunch, Claire,' Mum said as she packed brightly coloured sandwiches into my lunch box. Compensation. I wanted to hide them in a remote part of the farthest kitchen cupboard so that they'd grow horrible green mould and stink the place out when the plastic lid was removed. Revenge. 'Yes, when she's gone,' I thought, 'I'll hide them. There's no way I'm taking the sandwiches to school.'

That Friday morning in registration I felt like a Jehovah's Witness who sits quietly in the corner, missing the pre-vaccination excitement and anticipation. No bared arm, no stories of previous needles that made a person faint – just a quiet corner and reading book, trying to ignore what was going on, trying to appear above it all.

Desks were covered with sepia photographs of army days and street parties. 'That's my grandad, the one in the middle,' someone said. Giggles. 'Didn't they look funny, the way they used to dress?'

'This is my great-grandparents on their wedding day.'

'Why didn't your great-grandma wear a proper wedding dress?'

'There wasn't enough white material available, my gran said.'

'That's my grandad in an army pantomime.'

Such excitement. It made me sick. Esme knew about my project – I'd told her the day before, after my mum had met Miss Sanders. She kept her folder closed and looked around at the other photographs and souvenirs without even mentioning her project.

Ruth paraded up and down the classroom like a visiting dignitary, commenting on the finished projects. 'Where's yours then?' she asked.

I knew exactly what I was going to say. My reply was well rehearsed. Through the night's rainstorm I had practised this scene over and over in my mind.

'Well?' Ruth asked again. Her loud, haughty inquiry silenced the buzz of excitement. All the questioning faces in the class turned to me. I knew exactly what I was going to do.

Slowly and deliberately I reached down to undo my schoolbag. I hadn't opened it since yesterday. The exciting sandwiches were safely at the back of the saucepan cupboard, steadily rotting into a smelly green mould.

I knew this plan well. 'Oh no!' I said with exaggerated disappointment. Then I was going to say, 'I don't believe it, I must have left it on the shelf next to the front door where I put it last night so that I wouldn't forget it this morning.'

That was the plan. But to my amazement, when I opened my schoolbag, the project was there, carefully placed alongside my other books. I was so shocked I could hardly lift it from the bag. Esme nudged me gleefully.

'Too ashamed to show us, are we?' Ruth said, smugly.

'No!' I shouted at Ruth before taking the project out. 'I'm not ashamed of my grandad. I'm really, really proud of him!'

'Good for you, Claire!' Jamie cheered from behind. Ruth stomped back to her desk as the class continued with their comparisons and questions. Miss Sanders was late – again.

On the front of my project folder was a message written on a yellow 'Stick-It' notice:

If you were as nosy as me, you'd know where she hides all the Christmas presents and banned projects! She won't miss it for one day.

Chris.

P.S. I have taken your sandwiches too – otherwise they'd go mouldy.

I couldn't stop smiling as I stroked each page of Grandad's precious story. 'That's my grandad outside his home in County Mayo, the day before he came to England and that's Roddy next to him,' I said, almost chuckling over the words.

'Don't they look funny with hair?' Esme said. We laughed – it was such a relief.

29

Grandad was right. All the fuss about my project did blow over very quickly because something much, much more important (or dreadful) happened.

Grandad died early on the Saturday morning.

Dad was with him and the parish priest. And Roddy. Roddy came for breakfast at our house. He sat quietly, his head almost permanently bowed. He watched distastefully as Mum grilled the bacon and poached the eggs.

It was a dreadful day. I'll never forget the awful ache at the bottom of my stomach which welled up into tears every few minutes. Every time I thought of Grandad, the last time I'd seen him at his home, with the blanket wrapped around his shoulders, I felt cold and so alone.

That awful ache seemed to churn over and roll itself into a tight knot when I thought of the last time I'd seen Grandad – in the hospital. I had been so horrible to him. All I'd wanted was for Grandad to straighten his mouth and talk properly.

If someone had told me that Grandad would soon . . . I would have said . . . well, I would have hugged him. The ache pushed upwards into my ribs when I thought of all the times I'd nagged Grandad to tell me his story. All the times I had said, 'Why weren't you ordinary like everybody else?'

I wish that I'd said goodbye.

Dad was busy all day arranging things. Mum answered the door to Grandad's friends, who wanted to say, 'I'm sorry for your trouble.' She was pale, harassed and a little confused.

'This is the way the Irish do things,' Roddy explained to my mum. 'They lift you up, let you know they care and keep you going just when you need the most support.' Roddy sat in the corner of our lounge, checking his hands and the racing pages for hours. His mouth quivered and shook but he didn't cry. He probably wanted to wait until he was back in his own home.

The computer was silent. 'Not today,' Dad said, terminating the bleeping invaders suddenly. 'Out of respect for your grandad.' Dominic and Chris didn't reply.

Does everybody think the same when their grandad dies? 'If only,' I kept thinking. If only Grandad had lived for one more day, walking and talking normally. If only he was sitting in his chair with his Woodbines and flapjack and hot chocolate just for one more hour, I'd be able to tell him all that had happened. How Chris had decided there was no point arguing with Mum over the project. 'Just nick it when she's not looking,' he decided. 'If she's at work Mum won't miss it for one day.' He knew where to look – being nosy, like he said. He knew all the hiding-places.

I'd tell Grandad about how Miss Sanders was delighted to see my mum had changed her mind and then disappointed when I told her the truth at the end of the lesson, when Ruth was safely out of the way. 'I'll have to take it home so that Chris can put it back.'

Miss Sanders was understanding when I expressed my worry at what people would say when my project wasn't in the exhibition. 'They won't notice,' she said confidently. 'They'll be so busy looking for their own masterpiece, they won't notice anyone else's. It's a shame though, Claire – it's such a good story. Such a different perspective on the war.'

Grandad would probably say, 'She's some teacher, that Miss Sanders,' in just the same way as he used to say, 'She's some girl, that Esme!'

It was a shame, as Miss Sanders had said – but it was even more than that. I almost felt annoyed with Miss Sanders because she wasn't as angry as I was – with Mum. Why couldn't we display Grandad's story? Why did Mum still find it so shameful? As Grandad had said to me right at the start – he was an ordinary person too. That's what the exhibition was about, ordinary men and women in the Second World War.

The church was packed to the doors for Grandad's funeral and that seemed to help the ache in the pit of my stomach. Dominic did the first reading. He stood up so proudly, the hypocrite. Although my dad had asked us not to argue and to be kind to one another, I couldn't help wishing Dominic would slip on the steps up to the lectern and bang his head. I wanted him to look a fool in his grown-up suit.

When the parish priest spoke, the ache seemed to disappear completely. He said that Grandad was a brave man who'd been a courageous miner during the war. 'He helped to keep things ticking over, while the other lads were away fighting.' I was so proud of my grandad that I wanted to jump up and pat him on the back. Then, out of the corner of my eye, I spotted the polished wooden coffin and the ache returned.

He was brave, my grandad, and good and kind. You just had to read to the very end of his story.

My Family and Other Natural Disasters

by Josephine Feeney

'You haven't got a life story.
You're only thirteen!'
'Mum, I've got thirteen years.'
'Well, you write your life story.
Just keep me out of it.'

Patrick Connolly is in trouble. He has to write his life story as a school project, but how can he when the Connollys are in the midst of a major family crisis and no one will answer his questions? Why do the adults in his life have to behave so ridiculously?

Set in Essex and the west of Ireland, this is a hugely entertaining bitter-sweet comedy.

The Revenge of the Demon Headmaster

by Gillian Cross

Hunkymania has hit the country. Suddenly
everyone is desperate to buy disgusting Hunky
T-shirts, trainers like pigs' trotters and pigswill
yoghurt. Only Dinah isn't mesmerized by the
craze. And when she and SPLAT set out to
investigate, they come face to face with their old
rival, the Demon Headmaster! It's a race against
time. Can they stop him carrying out the final act
of his demonic plan?

The Prime Minister's Brain

by Gillian Cross

Everyone at school is playing the new computer game, Octopus Dare – but only Dinah is good enough to beat it.

As it begins to take hold of her, Dinah realizes that the Octopus is trying to control her and the other Brains in the Junior Computer Brain of the Year Competition.

Why is it happening, and how is the Demon Headmaster involved? And what is the reason for wanting to get into the Prime Minister's Brain? Find out in this exciting and compulsive thriller.

READ MORE IN PUFFIN

For children of all ages, Puffin represents quality and variety – the very best in publishing today around the world.

For complete information about books available from Puffin – and Penguin – and how to order them, contact us at the appropriate address below. Please note that for copyright reasons the selection of books varies from country to country.

On the worldwide web: www.puffin.co.uk

In the United Kingdom: Please write to *Dept. EP, Penguin Books Ltd, Bath Road, Harmondsworth, West Drayton, Middlesex UB7 0DA*

In the United States: Please write to *Consumer Sales, Penguin USA, P.O. Box 999, Dept. 17109, Bergenfield, New Jersey 07621-0120*. VISA and MasterCard holders call 1-800-253-6476 to order Penguin titles

In Canada: Please write to *Penguin Books Canada Ltd, 10 Alcorn Avenue, Suite 300, Toronto, Ontario M4V 3B2*

In Australia: Please write to *Penguin Books Australia Ltd, P.O. Box 257, Ringwood, Victoria 3134*

In New Zealand: Please write to *Penguin Books (NZ) Ltd, Private Bag 102902, North Shore Mail Centre, Auckland 10*

In India: Please write to *Penguin Books India Pvt Ltd, 706 Eros Apartments, 56 Nehru Place, New Delhi 110 019*

In the Netherlands: Please write to *Penguin Books Netherlands bv, Postbus 3507, NL-1001 AH Amsterdam*

In Germany: Please write to *Penguin Books Deutschland GmbH, Metzlerstrasse 26, 60594 Frankfurt am Main*

In Spain: Please write to *Penguin Books S. A., Bravo Murillo 19, 1° B, 28015 Madrid*

In Italy: Please write to *Penguin Italia s.r.l., Via Felice Casati 20, I–20124 Milano*

In France: Please write to *Penguin France S. A., 17 rue Lejeune, F–31000 Toulouse*

In Japan: Please write to *Penguin Books Japan, Ishikiribashi Building, 2–5–4, Suido, Bunkyo-ku, Tokyo 112*

In South Africa: Please write to *Longman Penguin Southern Africa (Pty) Ltd, Private Bag X08, Bertsham 2013*